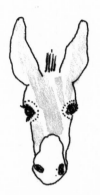

THE WHITE UMBRELLA
Brian Sewell

ILLUSTRATED BY SALLY ANN LASSON

David R. Godine, *Publisher*
BOSTON

Published in 2018 by
DAVID R. GODINE, Publisher, Inc.
Post Office Box 450
Jaffrey, New Hampshire 03452
www.godine.com

First published in 2015 by Quartet Books Limited
Text © Brian Sewell 2015
Illustrations © Sally Ann Lasson 2015

All Rights Reserved.
No part of this book may be used or reproduced in any manner whatsoever
without written permission from the publisher, except in the case of brief
quotations embodied in critical articles and reviews. For more information,
please write to: Permissions, David R. Godine, Publisher,
15 Court Square, Suite 320, Boston, Massachusetts 02108.

LIBRARY OF CONGRESS CATALOGING-IN-PUBLICATION DATA

Sewell, Brian, author. | Lasson, Sally Ann, illustrator.
The White Umbrella / Brian Sewell ; illustrated by Sally Ann Lasson.
Jaffrey, New Hampshire : David R. Godine, Publisher, 2018. | Originally
published: London : Quartet Books Limited, 2015. | Summary: Mr. B,
an English historian in Pakistan working on a documentary, spies
a young donkey that has been abused and, leaving his film crew
behind, sets out to take the donkey to his home in London.
LCCN 2018010935 | ISBN 9781567926248 (hardcover : alk. paper) |
CYAC: Voyages and travels—Fiction. | Donkeys—Fiction.
LCC PZ7.1.S466 Whi 2018 | DDC [Fic]—DC23
LC record available at https://lccn.loc.gov/2018010935

FIRST U.S. EDITION

Written with Hoffmann's Nicklausse at one elbow,
Blaise Cendrars at the other, and on my conscience still,
that donkey in Peshawar.

CHAPTER 1

Mr B Rescues a Donkey Foal

MR B, A WIRY LITTLE MAN of fifty with white hair, was sitting in the back of a big white Land Rover when he saw the donkey. It was early evening and the dense rush-hour traffic in Peshawar was moving at a snail's pace—which was just as well, for Mr B suddenly opened the door, leaped down onto the road and, without a word, sprinted away between the carts and lorries, the buses and the motorcycles.

His companions, a television crew from London—for Mr B was in northern Pakistan to make a film about that country's ancient history—were taken by surprise. Dominic, the youngest and least important of them, but the

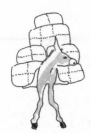 

tallest and the most willowy, had the sense to jump out too and run after Mr B. They did not much like him. He was serious and knew a great deal of ancient history, but he failed to understand that in making programmes for television what he knew was of absolutely no importance and that, as a presenter, he was no more than the puppet of the director and the cameraman.

Within two days of reaching Pakistan they were hardly speaking to each other. The cameraman was only interested in filming the brightly-painted trucks and lorries that constantly thundered past with passengers clinging to anything that offered support for hand or foot. The director, if they encountered a buffalo or camel, at once ordered Mr B to clamber on its back; he was also compelled to eat food offered in the street or play musical instruments. Mr B, however, knowing that two thousand, three hundred years earlier Alexander the Great, the most formidable of heroes in the history of Ancient Greece, had marched his armies all the way from Macedonia to Pakistan, was anxious to know if any traces of that conquest still survived in modern language, customs or culture. Most of all he would have liked to find a fierce Pakistani warrior in the remoter regions of the Hindu Kush, capable of conversing with him in Ancient Greek – but for two long weeks Mr B had been allowed to find nothing of the kind and now was boiling over with frustration.

That they called him Mr B was an indication of the rift between them. Feeling deeply unfriendly toward him, they did not want to use his first name, and to have turned to the formality of his surname might have suggested that they held him in high respect for his knowledge – which was far from the case. It was young Dominic who, if truth be told, liked and respected him very much and perfectly understood the anguish that he felt when the programme that he had hoped to make faded into oblivion, who began to address him as Mr B, and then the others took it up. To call him Mr B was not aggressively unfriendly, yet suggested a certain distance, and Dominic could make it seem genuinely affectionate.

When Dominic caught up with Mr B, he found him with his arm around the neck of a tiny donkey, dabbing his handkerchief in four deep wounds on her back, from which flowed strong trickles of blood. These had been caused by a wicker 'saddle' used in Pakistan to provide a flat platform for the enormous loads that donkeys are often forced to carry. But this donkey, Dominic could at once see, was far too young to work. He could also see that Mr B was magnificently angry. 'I doubt if she is six months old. She may still be drinking her mother's milk. Any fool can see that the bones and joints of her legs are not properly formed....'

At this point the fat director and the cameraman, panting and drenched with sweat, arrived. Dominic explained. 'Leave the donkey and get back into the car,' demanded the director. 'Not without the donkey,' said Mr B, 'I can't and won't just leave her here.' As they argued, the volume of their voices rose and a ring of uncomprehending spectators formed about them. Reason dictated that they should leave the donkey to her fate and drive on to Islamabad where, next day, they were to board a plane to Heathrow, but Mr B was not a reasonable man — indeed, when provoked, he could be a most unreasonable man. 'We'll leave you,' threatened the fat director. 'Do,' Mr B replied with remarkable force and clarity for such a short and simple word. The cameraman took his arm, but Mr B shook him off. 'What will you do if we leave you?' asked Dominic very quietly. 'Walk home,' said Mr B, 'with the donkey,' a broad grin spreading over his face.

For a whole hour they wrangled and the crowd, bored by an argument in which no one was murdered or even came to blows, thinned until only Mr B and the television crew were left. Night fell, but not even the chill of darkness dented Mr B's determination. In the end Dominic fetched Mr B's luggage from the car and, into a small and comfortable knapsack that had been his companion on many earlier journeys and long-distance walks, helped him to pack only what was really useful. Into it went his sponge bag, scissors shaped for cutting fingernails, a fresh notebook, spare pens and everything that might keep him warm and dry. He remembered too to bring Mr B's umbrella – no ordinary umbrella, but one of strong white canvas on a frame of metal ribs exquisitely engineered about a stock as heavy as the strongest walking-stick, specially made for him ten years before, hardly a stone's throw from the British Museum, by James Smith and Sons (and Grandsons, Great-Grandsons and more and more, for they made their first umbrella in 1830, the year that William IV came to the throne). The canvas was no longer white, for this was an umbrella that had crossed the Sahara and its sand-storms when Mr B was searching there for evidence of prehistoric human occupation, that had been with him in Pompeii and furthest Sicily, indeed everywhere from

Barcelona to Baghdad, and had proved to be the Rolls-Royce of umbrellas.

'What shall we tell them when we get back to London?' asked the director, still not quite believing that this was about to be the parting of their ways.

'Tell them the truth – that I found a baby donkey and I am walking home with it.'

'You are mad,' said the director.

'Perhaps,' said Mr B, 'but it is a decent sort of madness of which you are incapable. We shall see you in a year or so.'

To this the director ungraciously replied, 'I don't care if I never see or hear of you again. You and your damned donkey.'

Dominic, last to return to the Land Rover, gave Mr B a hug and whispered, 'I'll tell the Foreign Office – and Mrs B, of course.'

CHAPTER 2

Farooq the Pharmacist

S O THERE WAS MR B, shivering a little in the cold that tumbles down on Peshawar from the Himalayas so that, though by day the temperature can be roasting hot to an Englishman, by night it can be as cold as Christmas. All this time the donkey foal had stood close to him, pressing, much as big dogs often do against their master's thighs. Feeling her shiver too, he pulled his one warm wind-cheating garment from his knapsack and, knotting the sleeves about her neck, just about covered her shoulders with it; then, taking the old leather belt from his trousers, soft with long use, he slipped this too about her neck like a dog collar and lead. All but one of the shops nearby had closed, but a bright light announced the exception to be a PHARMACY, and that was exactly what Mr B wanted.

He and the donkey crossed the road and stood politely at the door, for Mr B thought that a pharmacist might not be happy to have a donkey in his shop. When he called 'Good evening' to anyone who might be in its depths, an old man with a neatly trimmed beard came to the door. Mr B explained that he wanted something to disinfect the four wounds in the donkey's back, and then something more to protect them from flies as they healed. The old man was amused. He was so old that he could remember when Pakistan and India were one vast undivided country and it all belonged to the British Empire; he was so old that he had been to schools that were as English as any ancient grammar school in England and spoke a form of English as refined, grammatical and precise as Mr B's; and he was so old that he knew perfectly well that the English can be obstinate in their affection for animals. His name was Farooq—which mightily amused Mr B, who had once encountered, when young and foolish, a deposed king of Egypt who bore that name; but to speak of this, he realised, was quite irrelevant and he kept his memory to himself.

Farooq instructed Mr B to take the donkey round the block to his back door, where the tumble-down shop declined into the lean-to shack that was its storeroom; there he would tend her wounds. He swabbed them clean, deftly closed them with stitches (with not a whimper from the donkey – but then animals often instinctively know when humans are being kind to them, even if it hurts), and covered them with patches to keep the flies away. He thought she was perhaps only three or four months old, had certainly not finished drinking her mother's milk, should never have been made to carry a load, and then he delivered his surprise – 'You realise, of course, that she is far too young to walk four thousand miles. You will have to carry her.' Though he said this with laughter in his voice and eyes, he could not have been more serious.

Farooq was Mr B's first stroke of luck. Before the evening was much older the pharmacist was making lists of things that would be good for the donkey to eat, and of other things that would upset her tummy. He stressed how much water she should drink – clean water from a bucket, not dirty water from a roadside pool. And he told Mr B that she should, as far as possible, walk in the shade – as, in nature, she would

walk in the shade cast by her mother – and should not walk more than five miles in a day, and those five never in one unbroken journey. There were other instructions, among them a blanket to keep her warm at night, something waterproof to keep her dry in storms and perhaps a hat to shade her head, and as the list grew longer Mr B began to realise that his first assumption, that she would carry his luggage while he held the umbrella over them both and they walked twenty miles a day, was far from what was really to happen.

'How do you know so much about donkeys?' asked Mr B.

'Oh I'm so old that I date back to the time before the car was everywhere, when every family had a donkey or two and we children all had to look after them. My mother always did her shopping on a donkey, and I and my brothers, when we were very small, often sat in front of her when she trotted off to market. Without cars the air in Peshawar was much cleaner in those days, but life could be very tough and short for donkeys, for almost all were made to work too hard. Your donkey, if you succeed in getting her to England, may be yours for thirty years. Our donkeys often lived to be ten or so, but most others were worked to death by five.'

'You must think me mad,' said Mr B.

'Not so,' replied Farooq with a wry smile as he set about trying to make a bed of sorts for the donkey with flattened cardboard boxes and other packing material. 'Shall we say eccentric? Now she must dine on what fruit and vegetables I have, and we too must have some supper.'

Farooq lived over the shop, the only member of his family to do so, for his wife had died many years before and his sons had better things to do than run a twenty-four-hour pharmacy. 'It is what I do,' he said when Mr B gently enquired why, at eighty, he chose to work so many hours. 'What else should I do? It is because I provide a service that we are having this conversation. Is that not good? Is that not better for you than finding the shop shut and your not knowing what to do with your sad little donkey until morning?' Then he offered Mr B a bed, but he, having in his mind determined that he would keep company with the donkey if Farooq was not offended, refused it and instead stretched out on the shed floor among the cardboard boxes, next to the donkey, just as he did with his dogs in London – though there they were all on his big and very comfortable bed.

Mr B woke early, aching in every joint, and the donkey, hearing him get up, got up herself, unsteadily. She was, he realised, a bag of bones in which, when he ran his fingers over her skin, he could count every rib, her wobbly legs absurdly long supporting a body that at this stage was no bigger than that of an Alsatian dog. He measured every animal by the big Alsatian bitch waiting for him at home and, lifting the donkey (which she seemed not to mind), he thought their weights much the same. Outside, in the clear morning light, he saw how pretty she was, her coat as soft and silky as a whippet's – and he had a whippet at home too, matching her in exactly the same range of colours as the milkiest of coffees. 'With those long legs you have the makings of a ballet dancer,' he said to himself, 'and I shall call you Pavlova – Little Miss Pavlova until you grow up.' And his mind wandered with thoughts of another Pavlova, the other Pavlova, indeed, Anna Pavlova, a beautiful Russian ballet dancer who died on the day that Mr B was born, still so famous that balletomanes who could never have seen her dance and knew her artistry only from scratched and creaking films in black and white, still speak of her with awe.*

* For Anna Pavlova, PAV-loh-vuh is the pronunciation pre-
ferred in ballet circles. The anglicised pav-LOH-vuh should
be used only for the pudding that bears her name.

When Farooq appeared with breakfast for Pavlova – a bale of fresh hay – he said, 'I have good news for you. A friend is driving to Quetta to-morrow to collect some stores for me and will take you with him. It will knock some five hundred miles off your journey, but it com-mits you to going south and then west-north-west across Persia – but only one border to cross. If you go north the journey is much shorter, but you may cross and re-cross a dozen borders, some of them – Afghanistan, Kashmir, Russia – dangerous and unpredicta-ble. Any of these might mean arrest for you, and were you to be separated from your donkey, it would almost certainly be the end for her.'

Mr B wished that he had a map – and, indeed, he had one in his head, but all that he could clearly remember was that the great mountain-ous mass of Afghanistan (never a safe place for a solitary Englishman) was in the way. The sim-plicity of Farooq's longer journey appealed to him, for not only did it avoid the hard climbing and bitter cold of the mountains of the Hin-du Kush (lower only than the Himalayas into which they run), he had only one (though rather large) country to cross before reaching the Turkish border, and in Turkey he had friends. 'Come,' said Farooq, 'we must go shopping for the journey.'

They bought a small plastic bucket from which Pavlova could drink, two flat plastic water-bottles as an emergency supply, and a pair of simple saddlebags cut from old kilim rugs (and rather pretty) so that she could carry her own baggage. A bootmaker made a broad leather collar for her and a lead for Mr B to hold. A tailor made a coat for her from a heavy blanket, adapted an old army groundsheet into a waterproof overall, and trimmed a plump sheepskin to act as a saddle—there were to be no more holes in Pavlova's beautiful skin. Mr B ruined several straw hats (and paid for them) before he worked out where and how to cut holes through which to pull her ears, and for himself he bought a big blanket that he could fold into a cushion and in which he could wrap himself and Pavlova at night. With another bale of fresh hay and a box of fruit and vegetables Mr B was convinced that the journey to Quetta would be effortless and comfortable.

It was not. Again they slept together in the shack, trying some of their purchases, and Mr

B was not quite so creaky when, very early, Farooq wakened them so that Pavlova could have some exercise before being lifted onto the truck. With a bread and honey breakfast Mr B felt ready for anything until he saw the truck; it was very old, very rusty and rather small—the kind of truck left behind by the British Army when Pakistan gained her independence in 1947. Pavlova and Mr B scrambled into the back under what used to be called a 'tilt'—a canvas cover like a tent supported on a flimsy metal frame—there to protect the truck's load from the elements and, less successfully, from the

dust and stones thrown up by the rear wheels; in army parlance such a truck became known as a 'tilly'. Mr B settled himself as best he could, supported by his knapsack and the folded blanket, while Pavlova lay on her sheepskin, resting her head on his knees; the driver had wanted to hobble her ankles to prevent her from jumping out, but Mr B, imagining the dreadful cramps that this might cause, would not allow it. The driver and his mate, of course, were far more comfortable in the front cabin, but they did remember from time to time that Pavlova and Mr B, bouncing about in the back, needed occasionally to get out and stretch their legs.

The journey to Quetta took two whole days. The truck bucked, rattled and creaked along a rough road that at one moment climbed bare mountains, and at another ran along river valleys fertile with the rich crops of autumn. When they came to wayside places where they could buy tea and bread, fruit and milk, the driver stopped and helped Mr B to unload Pavlova so that she could walk a little, nibble fresh bread and even drink a bucket of fresh milk instead of water. It was in one of these places, where the driver and his mate knew that they could find a bed, that they spent the night, though their passengers resolutely curled up together under the tilt, not quite protected from the bitter mountain cold. On the second day they reached Quetta too late to seek out Farooq's suppliers, and again slept under the tilt, but not before having a merry farewell supper with the driver and his mate, at a restaurant in the open air where no one seemed to mind the presence of a donkey at the table.

CHAPTER 3

The Accidental Drug Trafficker

PAVLOVA SLEPT well enough on her dense sheepskin, but in the square space under the tilt Mr B had a second uncomfortable night, unable, even diagonally, to straighten his legs, nor, when curled on his side, could he find soft spots for his shoulder and his hip; moreover the whole floor seemed covered with jagged steel projections as sharp as dragon's teeth. When the driver and his mate woke him to say their farewells, collect Farooq's supplies and return to Peshawar, he was not in the best of moods; for two days the tilly's rear wheels had pelted him with dust and stones; for two days he had not showered or shaved or changed his clothes, and now he, Pavlova and their luggage were being unloaded onto the street where he could not even sluice his face in cold water. Instead, he slapped his cheeks to make the blood flow a little faster, ran his fingers through his tousled hair, emptied what reserved water they had into Pavlova's bucket, and then both he and she breakfasted on apples, sweet and crisp.

All this done, at least his teeth felt clean.

Having thus far pulled himself together he set off to find the market and replenish their supplies – not difficult, for markets are busy, noisy places and though he was not aware of it, Pavlova's nose was twitching with anticipation as, very discreetly, she steered him toward it. There he found fresh milk for her, still warm from the cow, which she at once drank from her bucket, and even a bale of fresh hay, perfumed with wild flowers, that would keep her happy for a day or two, and they found a fountain from which they could replenish their empty water bottles. Water, however, is heavy to carry, and so are fruit and vegetables, and poor Mr B found himself uncomfortably laden when, at last, most of their purchases were stowed in plastic bags awkwardly swinging from his knapsack. He felt like a tramp; unwashed, he was as grubby as a tramp; and only the cut of his clothes and the magnificence of his umbrella prevented his being mistaken for a tramp.

It was when, still in the centre of the city, Mr B asked to be directed to the road into Persia that he realised how alone he was and how far he had to go, for no one seemed to understand him until the fifth or sixth man whom he asked, and he it was who roared with laughter at the question – though not unkindly. 'Persia,' he said, 'is five hundred miles away and you would be wiser to ask for the first town or village on the road. Of a stranger standing in Trafalgar Square would you ask the way to Edinburgh?' Mr B, astonished to encounter in the middle of nowhere (as astonished people say) a man who, in perfect English, spoke to him of home, murmured an apology and then added, 'But I really need to know.' Given the direction and, for good measure, the information that in a straight line he and Pavlova were still as far from London as they had been in Peshawar, Mr B again recognised how alone he was, how much he had to do and how long it would take if Pavlova could walk only five miles in a day. This was only the fifth day since he had stood in the middle of the traffic in Peshawar with his arm about her neck, a terrified and trembling donkey foal, yet he felt that he had been with her for weeks, the bond between them quite unbreakable; yet he also felt, now that there was no Farooq to guide him further on his way, that he had been an impulsive fool. When he saw a bus destined for Karachi, Pakistan's chief seaport, where he could so easily take a plane to London, the impulse to board it and leave Pavlova where she stood with her saddlebags and sheepskin was, for a moment, irresistible.

Then his fond madness suddenly returned. He looked at Pavlova, her pretty eyelashes, her pale and silken coat, her long and knobbly legs, faintly ridiculous with her ears poking through her straw hat, and he had no doubt that he must at least attempt to achieve his original intention to take her back to London. With reinforced resolve he opened his big white umbrella and, with Pavlova's lead shortened, bringing her very close to his side, sharing the shade, they set off towards the west and the Persian border, a hundred days away if Farooq was right about the five mile daily limit on Pavlova's walking. To amuse himself (and, perhaps, Pavlova) he began to sing, softly at first, something about walking across meadows that he much

less than half remembered from the days before his voice broke, by César Franck, a French composer killed in Paris in 1890 when he was run over by a horse-bus. Recalling this calamity, Mr B walked towards the on-coming traffic with Pavlova on his inner side, so that he could push her out of the way if any of the many monster trucks threatened to run them down. And soon enough one did, a huge and hideous nemesis of a truck of precisely the type that the television cameraman had so often filmed, its horn blaring but its driver making no attempt to avoid them. In disbelief Mr B left it almost too late before giving Pavlova an almighty shove into the dirty ditch that ran beside the road, tumbling in on top of her.

Fortunately the ditch, though dirty, was not deep, and though they lay in it for a minute, knocked breathless, they were not unpleasantly filthy when they scrambled out. Some straightening of saddlebags was necessary and several of the plastic bags of fruit and vegetables had split, but the hay was still dry (donkeys hate wet hay) and what mud clung to the umbrella would soon brush off. A hundred yards along, on the other side of the road, a battered people-carrier had stopped, its driver having seen the accident. 'Everything all right?'

he asked when Mr B was alongside. 'Bit shaken,' said Mr B, 'but nothing broken. Kind of you to ask – but why did you assume that I am English?' The driver laughed. 'It's the umbrella – all the English had them in the years before Independence. Now we never see them and only people as old as me remember them. Why don't you hop in? This is no place for a morning walk.'

'What about my donkey?' asked Mr B.

'She can go in the back.'

'I'd be very glad of a lift, but only if I'm in the back with her.'

And so, with some folding of seats and shifting of luggage, room was soon made for Mr B as well as Pavlova, and they were on their way to Zahedan, the first city across the Persian border, five hundred miles away along the Chagai Hills that form the border between Pakistan and Afghanistan. The landscape was very beautiful, ever-changing and awe-inspiring, but the road was even rougher than that between Peshawar and Quetta, and very soon poor Pavlova was sick on Mr B's trousers. The driver, whose name was Zulfikar, pulled up where a mountain spring trickled down the rock face as though it were an infant waterfall; then, lifting Pavlova from the back, he led her to it, encouraged her to drink, and then took her for a short walk while Mr B, having removed his shoes, stood close to the trickling water so that it could run down his trousers and flush away all trace of Pavlova's breakfast.

Standing there with the sun on his back to remind him of the midday heat that would beat down on them within an hour or two, and deeply worried by Pavlova's sudden travel sickness, Mr B decided on a change of plan.

'We can't go on like this,' he said when Zulfikar returned, 'you've been very kind but we cannot stop every twenty miles when you have business to do five hundred miles away. You should drive on. We shall rest here until the sun goes down and then walk on by night, resting from time to time. With luck we might manage ten miles before the sun rises again.'

'Then it will take you fifty days to reach Zahedan,' Zulfikar replied, 'or not reach it at all, for in the pitch dark you are likely to be flattened by some weary driver half asleep at the wheel. No, no—we shall rearrange things in the van so that you and the donkey are in the middle and not bouncing about in the back—you will both be far more comfortable and she will not be sick.'

Mr B thought this extraordinarily kind and

was persuaded to accept—but what he did not know was that Zulfikar's kindness was by no means the same generous unselfish kindness that Farooq had shown them, for the business that he had five hundred miles away in Zahedan was the delivery across the Persian border of fifty kilogrammes of heroin, a dangerous drug crudely distilled in Afghanistan and ultimately destined for western Europe where, because it is illegal there, the smugglers make great fortunes. Zulfikar was third in the chain of smugglers; it began with the farmers of Afghanistan who grew the poppies and made the first distillation of the drug; the second link was the group of peasants who drove laden donkeys just like Pavlova on narrow and dangerous paths through the mountains that form the southern border of that country; and Zulfikar and his people-carrier were the link between Pakistan and Persia. The odd thing was that he looked every bit the pantomime smuggler, for his nose was hooked, his eyebrows bushy and his moustache curled dramatically upward at its two extremities; moreover, he flashed his eyes and laughed too much, revealing more gold teeth than any gentleman would ever have; but it never occurred to Mr B that he had fallen into the hands of a deceitful rogue.

Zulfikar had made this journey many times and had learned that turning up at the border with all sorts of local travellers and their baggage was the best way of slipping past the guards without attracting notice; but the moment he saw Mr B and Pavlova he thought a change of camouflage might make sense, and when he saw them tumbled into the ditch, the chance of pretending to be their rescuer confirmed his plan. Everything about Mr B–and particularly the umbrella–told Zulfikar that he was English and, encumbered by a baby donkey, not exactly at ease walking along the road from Quetta. If he crossed the Persian border pretending that he was only a taxi driver hired to take Mr B wherever he wished, then, if there were difficulties with the guards he could protest that he knew nothing of the heroin, that it was Mr B's, not his; Mr B would then disappear for ever into a Persian prison, Pavlova would fall into the hands of some cruel slave-driver, and he, Zulfikar, if he stuck to his story, would lose the heroin but live to tell the tale. And so, laughing, smiling and talking too much, Zulfikar stuffed his cardboard boxes of heroin (all labelled 'Granulated Sugar') between the front and middle row of seats, and topped them with Pavlova's sheepskin and pretty saddlebags to make a comfortable platform from which she could see the passing landscape and occasionally sniff the breeze.

Mr B suspected nothing of Zulfikar's smiling treachery and the jeopardy in which he was; he was grateful that he was comfortably ensconced in the front seat, that he could easily reach over its back and stroke Pavlova were she to be disturbed by a particularly vicious bump in the road, and he was mightily relieved that she showed no further signs of being travel sick. They had a rather jolly evening in a village where a wedding was being celebrated and all who stopped were invited to the feast and, waking early the following morning, completed the journey to Zahedan before mid-afternoon. At the border Mr B showed his passport to the guard by reaching across Zulfikar, but the guard, taking it with his right hand and at the very same moment opening the rear door with his left to see whatever might be seen, disturbed Pavlova, who had been fast asleep. Startled from her drowsing, she raised her head and brayed, her lips drawn back, her teeth bared. Now, not once since Mr B had rescued her had Pavlova made a sound other than the faint clip-clopping of her hooves, but, alarmed, she did what donkeys do and emitted a harsh he-haw so loud that the guard, so close to it, was deafened. 'He-haw,' she said, and then 'he-haw' again and yet again. To find a donkey in a car was unexpected enough, but to have it, at such close quarters, making a noise as full-throated, ear-splitting and raucous as the maniacal laughter of some drunken Hercules, made the guard jump backward. Other guards, with guns, ran to see what

was amiss; when they looked into the car and saw only little Pavlova, they roared with laughter and called their mate a dunderhead; indeed, for weeks after they teased him with cries of 'He-haw, he-haw' – little knowing that they had missed the drug-haul of their lives. They also forgot to look properly at Mr B's passport and failed to notice that he had no permit to travel in Persia, but with broad smiles waved Zulfikar on towards the town of Zahedan.

CHAPTER 4

A Persian Poet and
a Persian Map

ZAHEDAN, though scruffy and flyblown, as many border towns in Asia are, proved to be a busy little city. Close to the westernmost point of Pakistan and the south-west corner of Afghanistan and, by road, connected with the Arabian Sea three hundred miles due south, it is something of an international trading-post for almost everything, legal and illegal. Zulfikar drove Mr B straight to the central market and there they parted, the best of friends, embracing, slapping each others' backs, Mr B trustingly oblivious of what might have happened at the border had the guards insisted on inspecting the luggage on which Pavlova lay when she let loose her hideous cry. Now she was happy to again be on her feet and many of the stall-holders, amused to see so English-looking an Englishman with his big white umbrella and a gangling adolescent donkey, gave her apples, quinces, grapes and other titbits as she passed.

At one stall, piled high with books, Mr B found a map of Persia. It was, of course, labelled IRAN, writ large, the name that officially replaced Persia in 1935. Mr B, however, like many of his generation, had since boyhood known the country by the name it bore in the time of his hero, Alexander the Great, and was disinclined ever to call it Iran; illogically, the official language is still referred to as Persian. Obviously intended for a schoolroom, on heavy waxy paper from which grubby finger marks could easily be removed with a damp cloth, this map showed all Persia's provinces distinguished in blocks of bright green and yellow, pink and purple, on which he could easily discover all the main towns and cities, all the major roads

and even – something of which he had not thought – occasional railways.

'Well I'll be damned,' he said on discovering that Zahedan was a railway terminal. 'I'll be damned.' 'What have you found?' enquired the young man whose stall it was, a sort of Persian Dominic, as tall and willowy as he but with the unfathomably dark eyes of a poet. 'I have come all the way from Quetta by road, and only now that I am here do I discover that I could have come by train,' said Mr B. 'By road?' said the poet. 'Then you, an Englishman with money in your pocket – for your splendid umbrella makes that obvious – are lucky to be alive. That road is the smugglers' road and they would cut your throat for a shilling.'

Mr B, who had never been good at even the simplest arithmetic, wanted to know the distance in miles. He could remember that eighty kilometres equal fifty miles, but with twenty-five, fifty and eighty rattling about his brain, could make no sense of the conundrum. The bookseller, realising that Mr B might be with him for some time, introduced himself as Mirzah and sent a barefoot boy of perhaps eight to bring them glasses of tea (tea in the east is always served in tiny glasses, without milk, but often sweetened with inordinately large doorsteps of sugar); he also presented Mr B with pencil and paper. 'Let me get the total distance in kilometres right,' said Mr B to Pavlova, 'and the miles will fall into place.' This was true, but he first multiplied twenty-five by seven, and then what seemed a not unrealistic answer by ten, and then divided that by eighty and somehow arrived at roughly twenty-two... at which point he was compelled to ask Pavlova, 'But twenty-two what?' Determined not to be defeated he tried again by going back to the beginning and argued that if each centimetre represented twenty-four kilometres instead of twenty-five, his calculation would be simpler, for twenty-four is three times eight, and if eight kilometres are the equivalent of five miles, then one centimetre must equal five multiplied by three – and that is fifteen miles. Thus the original measurement from south-east to north-west must equal a little less, because of reducing twenty-five to twenty-four (or might it be a little more?), than a thousand miles.

As no one ever travels in a straight line, poor Mr B was more than a little depressed to realise that the real distance he must travel must be much more than he had calculated. He had been with Pavlova for only seven days, but he felt deeply unwashed, creased, crumpled and exhausted; more than anything in the world he wanted to wash his clothes and stand under a streaming shower. He paid for the map and for a book on early Persian dynasties (a reminder of his enthusiasm for Alexander the Great) that Pavlova had half eaten while he was struggling with arithmetic, and then, just as he was saying goodbye to Mirzah, asked him if he knew of an hotel where he could stay with his donkey. A piercing whistle summoned the small boy who had brought them tea; Mirzah gave him instructions and off he went, leading Mr B by the hand. Down a narrow back street only a few minutes from the market, the boy leaned on a great and beautifully carved wooden door that opened onto a courtyard where several sheep were resting in the shade of a very old mulberry tree. 'This is an hotel?' asked Mr B, but the boy, who knew no English, did not answer – he merely took Pavlova's lead and looped it round a post, and then took Mr B up some dark stairs to a cool vestibule decorated with beautiful big tiles so exquisite in colour and pattern that they deserved to be in a museum. Coming in from the brilliant shafting sunlight of late afternoon, Mr B could hardly see the old white-bearded man seated in the shadows, with whom the boy, gesturing towards Mr B, began what seemed to be a long conversation.

It was, in fact, the instruction of Mirzah on Mr B's behalf, knowing that the old man spoke no English. 'Here is an Englishman,' said the boy, 'who is infatuated with a donkey. He needs a bath, clean clothes and somewhere safe to leave the donkey while he plans his journey, rests a little and goes to the bank. He will probably stay for two nights.'

The old man conducted Mr B to a quiet cool bedroom from which, to his great joy, he could see that Pavlova was safe, that some sensible and understanding soul had given her fresh

hay and let her loose to settle with the sheep. Then communicating by gesture, the old man showed Mr B the bathroom – again beautifully tiled – where water flowed into a deep marble basin from which the bather, seated on a bench, filled an ornate brass jug and poured the contents over himself. This is exactly what Mr B did for fully twenty minutes, the cold water reviving him, and then the old man brought him towels and took away his dirty clothes. In the clean shirt and trousers that he had tucked away in the bottom of his knapsack, perhaps a little too creased and crumpled to be described as smart, Mr B found his way to a bank and exchanged his Pakistani notes and some American dollars (always the easiest cash to change in remote and difficult places) for the Persian currency that he needed for the next and very long leg of his journey. He then returned to the market place to thank Mirzah for his help and suggest that they might have dinner together.

Mirzah was much more than a man who sold schoolbooks. He spoke all the local languages, Farsi (the official language), Azeri, Kurdish, Turkish and the Pashto and Dari of nearby Afghanistan, for this part of central Asia had long been an area of shifting borders and racial minorities. When Mr B and he sat in the garden of a restaurant there was at once a gathering of onlookers who begged Mirzah to recite the ancient love poems of Baluchistan, the province of which Zahedan was capital, and some of these he sang, the sweetness of his tenor voice hushing all within earshot. This, thought Mr B, could have happened at any time in the past two or three thousand years, for Persia had been a civilised empire when the Bible's Old Testament was young, its at times vast territory ranging from the Mediterranean Sea to the River Indus in Pakistan, rubbing shoulders (often angrily) with Ancient Greece and Rome, and neighbours even more ancient in what are now India and China. Did Alexander the Great, he wondered, sit in this very garden, under its lofty trees, listening to love songs sung by another such dark-eyed young poet? For many moments Mr B felt possessed by all that had happened in so long a past and heard none of the interrupting honks of passing motor cars; instead, he heard only the climbing range of Mirzah's melancholy voice (for all the best love songs are sad) and imagined it to be the echo of the first singer ever to sit at the feet of the first King of Kings, the title borne by all the monarchs of all the ancient dynasties of Persia.

Dinner done, parting imminent, they paused

for a moment to discuss the map. 'You have two choices,' said Mirzah; 'go north and then west along the shore of the Caspian Sea, or roughly along the straight line that you tried to measure earlier, but you must avoid the arid deserts of salt and sand that lie between them – cruel country for Pavlova if you have to walk. If you can get to Kerman, the capital of the next province to the west – perhaps two hundred and fifty miles, for the road loops far to the south – and then another sixty miles by road to Zarand, you can then take the train to Isfahan, and there you will be more than half way to Turkey.' 'Shall I be allowed to take a donkey on the train?' asked Mr B, and 'Wait and see,' said Mirzah who had again been implored to sing another song. They embraced, said their goodnights, and Mr B wandered off into the darkness, Mirzah's beautiful voice slowly fading in the still and starlit night.

Mr B and Pavlova rested for most of the next day. She was evidently at ease with the sheep in the courtyard and enjoyed the sweet mulberries that fell from the old tree, and he, apparently the only guest in the hotel, luxuriated in its cool tranquillity and the beauty of its tiles – 'When I get home,' he said to himself, 'I shall reconstruct the bathroom so that it exactly resembles this.' He took Pavlova for a long walk in the cool of the morning and again in the early evening, and bought her delicious things to eat (that is, delicious to a donkey, for Mr B had never eaten hay). Later in the evening he again had dinner with Mirzah, but when he said that he must go early to bed because he wanted to walk as far as Pavlova could before the sun rose too high, the poet begged him to stay a little longer – 'There is someone I want you to meet.' The someone was a small dark man who gave an impression of tireless energy – a bus driver. 'This is Fred,' said Mirzah. 'Fred?' enquired Mr B. 'Yes, I know' – Mirzah's voice took on the tone of resignation – 'it is not his real name but for many years he worked for Americans who could not pronounce any part of his Persian name, so they called him Fred – and now he prefers it; it has the virtue of one syllable instead of nine and is unique throughout at least two of this country's largest provinces; it is fame of a kind. He drives the bus to and fro between Zahedan and Kerman. If you will pay for two seats and a little extra for clearing up any mess that Pavlova may make, you may travel on his bus tomorrow. He leaves for Kerman at eight in the morning. The two front seats behind him, usually reserved for women travelling alone, will be reserved for you. Do not be late, but also do not be early for Fred does not want other passengers to grumble that one of the best seats is occupied by a donkey – it is best that she is seen by as few as possible.' This was such wonderful news that Mr B embraced both the poet and the driver, and in this extraordinary moment they all kissed each other on both cheeks.

Mr B rose early next morning and bathed yet again in the beautiful bathroom – 'Goodness knows,' he said to himself, 'when next I shall find myself in any sort of bathroom, let alone one as enchanting as this.' Returning to his room he found both his shirts and both his trousers freshly laundered, and the old man in the shadows, who seemed never to go to bed, brought him honey and bread straight from the oven for his breakfast. Mr B then paid the modest bill and discreetly tucked some notes under the candlestick that had been the only source of light at night, saying 'For the poor' – words that the old man did not know but which Mr B was sure he understood. Gravely they bowed to each other in old-fashioned courtesy, and Mr B went down to the yard to collect his donkey.

CHAPTER 5

Pavlova Takes the
Train to Isfahan

MR B COULD HAVE SWORN that Pavlova said a farewell to each of the sleepy sheep in turn, nose to nose exchanging a little puff of breath with them. Poor things—did they know that while she was happily riding on a bus they were to be taken to the abattoir and turned into mulberry-flavoured mutton chops? At the bus station there was a little crowd from which Mr B and Pavlova stood apart, as though waiting for some other bus. At precisely three minutes to eight Fred arrived, took Mr B's blanket and Pavlova's sheepskin from them to spread on the floor, while urging other passengers to hurry—and in the confusion of gossiping, stowing luggage and making themselves comfortable, no one noticed that Fred and Mr B had bundled a donkey under one of the best seats. They knew soon enough, for it was Fred's custom to pull into a stopping-place every two hours or so, signalling early to Mr B that he should get Pavlova to her feet, ready to

be first in the queue for yoghurt, fresh bread or tea, and long before the end of the journey the other passengers were being kind to Pavlova, giving her tit-bits to nibble, stroking her ears (which donkeys do not particularly like, though she bore it calmly enough), and patting her rump. An old lady banned to the very back of the bus with two pairs of grumpy chickens attracted no interest at all, so Mr B bought her an enormous bag of grapes which she fed to the fowls and herself quite indiscriminately. To Mr B's relief, at no point was Pavlova sick—though he kept her straw hat ready for such an emergency.

The journey took twelve hours at an average speed of twenty miles an hour or so, twisting and turning, bouncing about on the rough road, the vast and arid basin of salt and sand of Kavir-e-Lut always to the north. A line of poetry, 'Boundless and bare, the lone and level sands stretch far away,' slipped into Mr B's mind, but he could recover neither the rest of it nor the name of the poet who wrote it.* At some bleak points where there was neither water nor shade Mr B fervently hoped that the bus would not break down, for it was old, the engine noisy, the exhaust thick with burnt oil, and the gears very difficult to change – he could sometimes see the muscles in Fred's arm bulge as, with an almighty crunch, he forced the lever into a lower gear. But it did not break down, and at eight in the evening it rolled into the bus station at Kerman. And what did Mr B immediately see but a battered people-carrier, its driver holding a scruffy sheet of cardboard on which he had scrawled ZARAND, Mr B's next destination. Fred knew the driver (who had not one word of English) and did the deal for Mr B, who must pay for all three seats in the middle row and a little extra should Pavlova be sick or suffer some other mishap; when two other passengers joined them, off they set for Zarand and its railway station.

* The poet was Shelley and the poem *Ozymandias*.

'Yes,' said the sleepy clerk in the booking office, 'there is a train for Isfahan in the morning; it leaves at six o'clock.' He was so accustomed to English and American travellers turning up at odd hours (even at midnight, as it was then) wanting to go to Isfahan, that he could answer them in perfect English—though he did not recognise them as English themselves if they came from Liverpool or Birmingham. Nor, at first, did he understand Mr B's attempt to buy a ticket for a donkey. Bleary-eyed, for he had been on duty for almost twenty-four hours, he peered through his little window to see what Mr B was pointing at, and saw Pavlova with her sheepskin and saddlebags, plastic bucket and straw hat. He nodded, a little too vigorously (as is the wont of people conversing in languages they do not share) and, pushing another ticket under the glass, indicated that Mr B might sleep on a bench in the waiting-room. There Mr B found other travellers with animals – a goat, two sheep, a crate of chickens – and smiling a silent greeting to all who were not fast asleep, settled Pavlova close to the sheep, not on her sheepskin but on his blanket (in consideration of their sensibilities) and himself on her sheepskin on a bench.

That bench was the hardest, narrowest, most uncomfortable bed that he had had since he had rescued Pavlova – worse, even, than sleeping in the tilly – yet he slept enough and was alert enough at half-past five or so, and ready for the train when it shunted into the station. Following the other passengers with animals he saw that they loaded them in the guard's van at the rear and then went to the carriages. The guard helped Mr B lift Pavlova aboard and did not object when he indicated that he wished to stay with her, but even offered him some bales of hay that were to be delivered in Isfahan, with which, in the meantime, Mr B could construct an armchair that was much more luxurious than the bare benches in the passenger compartments.

It was what is called a 'stopping-train'—that is a train that over some three hundred and fifty miles not only stopped at every station, but slowed to a halt in the middle of a hundred nowheres for anyone who indicated that he was a would-be passenger. More sheep and goats were loaded, more chickens, a dozen pure white ducks, and by half-past midnight, when the train at last chugged into Isfahan, Pavlova was just one animal in a quite considerable menagerie. Mr B held her close while all the others were noisily unloaded, shielding her from the clamour and the shouts, and then, under the dim platform lights, lifted her carefully down onto her long and spindly legs. The guard then indicated that they should follow him and he took them to what is called a lairage—not in any way an hotel, but a scruffy barn of a place in which animals and their owners, caught roofless overnight, might rest in safety until the world wakes up.

And when the world did wake, Mr B was torn between his desire to press on towards Turkey and take another train, or two, or three (for he now found his map a mystifying labyrinth and the station's timetables utterly bewildering), and the urge to do what all sensible travellers do when they find themselves in places celebrated for their history – and that is to look about them, wander and explore. He knew Isfahan to be one of the most ancient, fabled, legendary and picturesque cities in the whole of Asia. As old as the Bible and Babylon, and for centuries the capital of Persia, it was, historically, a place of splendid palaces, mosques and caravanserais, set among gardens lavishly watered by rivers and canals – and a century ago it was famous for its more than two hundred public baths, all of them clad in tiles to rival those that had given him such solace and delight when bathing in Zahedan. And every schoolboy knows (and Mr B knew it too, of course) that Isfahan lay on the great Silk Route that had for at least two thousand years connected the merchants of China with those of Istanbul and Venice, carrying not only silk but spices, porcelain and carpets.

The thought of carpets solved the problem. Mr B knew a great deal about carpets – not the wall-to-wall fitted carpets of the airport and the modern western house, but the intricately designed and patterned rugs made by deft fingers and judged by the human eye, that were first imported into Europe certainly by the fifteenth century and perhaps considerably earlier. Then they were so precious that Europeans put them, not on the floor, but on tables where they could not be worn out by tramping feet, or chewed by dogs enchanted by the oriental smells that even now seem still to cling to them.

Thus it was that, torn between hurrying on and finding such a rug, Mr B succumbed to temptation. Having spent precisely two days and two nights in the same clothes in a bus that was as hot as an oven and a guard's van that smelt like a farmyard, he felt in no condition to bargain with a shrewd carpet dealer. Next to the station he found a public bath, though one without a single ornate tile. Two young men wearing only towels about their waists gave him a similar towel, took away his clothes and sat him on a marble bench and almost drowned him with water poured from buckets—first hot, then cold, then hot again. They washed his hair, scrubbed and scraped his body, stretched a towel on the floor, made him lie on it face down, and then, barefoot, stood on his ribs and shoulders until he could hear his tendons crack. Then they rinsed him clear of soapsuds, wrapped him in enormous towels and, with a cut-throat razor, shaved him; finally they plucked the hairs from his nostrils ('Ouch!' he yelped again and again), massaged his temples and laid him on a simple bed, bidding him rest. An hour later they brought him tea and his clothes, freshly laundered, dried, ironed and looking almost new; they had, moreover, polished his shoes—shoes that he himself had not polished since buying them two years before.

Thus smartened, Mr B collected Pavlova from the lairage where he had left her in the care of a bearded old man with a nanny-goat; now he left their luggage with him too and, taking only his umbrella and her hat, set off to make a nuisance of himself among the carpet shops. It is a general rule in the Near and Middle East that merchants and craftsmen of particular kinds should group together—wreck the exhaust or tyres of your car and in one street on the edge of town you will find all the garagistes who can repair them—and so it is with carpet vendors. Many in Isfahan sold only modern copies of antique designs, and in these Mr B was not remotely interested. Many, in turn, were not remotely interested in Mr B, a shabby man in shirtsleeves trailing a donkey on a lead, and did not welcome him (they failed to recognise the quality of his umbrella); and it was half way through the morning before he saw a really old rug in the window of what was evidently a really old shop in a slightly scruffy back street a little away from all the others. It was not well lit; he bent until his nose was touching the window, peering at the colour and the closeness of the weave, looking for damage and repair. The main field of colour was blue (comparatively rare), the decoration – a pomegranate tree growing in a vase – a harmonious mixture of soft reds and browns, all the dyes entirely natural. He thought it not quite as old as he would have liked – perhaps the peasants' nimble fingers were at work on it when Queen Victoria came to the throne in 1837 – and he had hoped to find a rug made in Isfahan, while this (pretty well a carpet in size at two metres by four) quite clearly came from Khotan in Sin-Kiang, the westernmost province of China, where the native people were the Uigurs when this carpet was made. It amused Mr B to think that this carpet, to reach Isfahan, had travelled five hundred miles further than he, though over much more difficult terrain and many, many more years.

He hesitated to go into the shop with Pavlova, but when an elderly man came to the door and said, unasked, 'Come in, come in, and bring the donkey too,' in he went. A boy of ten or so appeared and took Pavlova's rein. 'Where is he taking her?' Mr B asked anxiously, and his host pulled aside a curtain to reveal a shady yard behind the shop littered with wet carpets, bordered by a rippling stream – 'We clean our carpets by the age-old method of letting them lie for a week or so in running water and drying them in the shade.' This he said with a marked air of superiority, but followed with a very gentle 'Your donkey will be quite safe here,' and filled her bucket with water and gave her apples to eat. That done, the two men settled down to look at carpets and another boy appeared, perhaps fourteen or fifteen, and he and the younger boy dismantled a great heap of rugs, unfolding, re-folding and re-stacking as they went. All this took time and after a while the carpet dealer spoke sharply to the boys and they disappeared. 'They are my grandsons; they are bringing tea,' he said, and then, reaching out his hand, 'my name is Reza; what is yours?'

Eventually Mr B selected two rugs, one of which did indeed come from Isfahan, and the carpet from the window, but could not quite make up his mind which, if any, he should buy. Impressed by his discerning choice – for all three were of considerable age and fine museum quality – Reza asked what was troubling him. 'Well,' said Mr B, 'I have my donkey to look after and she already has enough to carry – and so have I. I can only think of taking the rugs, and that is barely practical, but the carpet is so beautiful that I don't want to leave it.'

'That is not a problem,' said Reza. 'I have a brother in Tabriz, and together with other dealers we often send carpets to the Grand Bazaar in Istanbul and to Europe, to friends and relatives who have shops in Berlin, Amsterdam, Milan and London—we are a kind of Mafia. So, trust me, and the rugs and the carpet will probably be delivered to your house in London before you yourself are there. I could offer you transport all the way, but there are certain risks that, shall we say, a white man with a donkey should not take.' 'Of course I trust you,' said Mr B and, old-fashioned as he was, he took his cheque book from the wallet of documents and cash that he kept close to his tummy in a canvas belt under his shirt, and wrote a cheque for the full amount. Handing it to Reza, he said, 'And now you must trust me.' Mr B's account was with no ordinary High Street bank, but with Coutts, a private bank in the Strand, within spitting distance of Trafalgar Square and the National Gallery where he spent so much time examining old carpets painted by old painters in old pictures. A splendid (but slightly absurd) palazzo of pepper-pot domes, marble floors, pot plants and uniformed guardians, the bank is at least as grand as the National Gallery and a great deal older–indeed, it has been the Royal Family's bank for three full centuries, though Mr B has never bumped into the Queen there, and that is just as well, for he tended to tease this place of much bowing and scraping by wearing his shabbiest clothes whenever he called to cash a cheque. And as Coutts' cheques are much larger and are more imposing than ordinary cheques, Reza thought, 'This is without doubt a cheque that I can trust,' as he tucked it safely into his pocket.

'Where are you going now?' he then asked Mr B. 'Back to the railway station to make sense of the timetables if I can, and see if I and my donkey can take a train to Tehran, and then to Tabriz, where I hope to cross the border in-to Turkey.' 'Then perhaps I can help you–it is the least I can do now that you have bought so much from me without once arguing over my prices. My son is driving to Tabriz tomor-row and could take you as his passenger.' 'But what about my donkey?' was Mr B's immediate reply. 'Oh she will be more comfortable than you–she will recline on a magic carpet just be-hind you, where you can reach and hold her collar if you wish. Can you be here by eight? It is a long way–two days or so–but the roads are much better the nearer they are to Tehran.

Mr B and Pavlova spent the rest of the day wandering in what little was left of ancient Isfahan, for time and people have made it almost unrecognisable to anyone reading an account of its beauty written by travellers a century ago. Now, alas, Mr B found relics of gardens and old waterways, and ruins of once wonderful buildings fallen into disuse, and quite often he sat in the shade musing in poetic contemplation, while Pavlova only sat. The truth is that Mr B, never having had a donkey, had not the foggiest idea of what sort of relationship they should develop. He had had dogs all his life and knew that with these he had to engage in conversation – they might not speak English, but he was certain that they always caught his meaning; he knew too that he must share food with them, walk and play games with them and let them share his furniture, particularly his bed. So far he had treated Pavlova very much as though she were a dog and to some extent as though she were a daughter but, sitting in the shade of a cedar tree that was at least two centuries old, it occurred to him that had she been a dog she would still be an immature puppy. From the very first moment, back in Peshawar, she had leaned against him, pressing against his

hip and thigh, and this she still did most of the time, particularly in such noisy public places as railway stations and bazaars. This she must have decided for herself, for he had never attempted to teach her by pulling sharply on her lead or collar as he might a dog. Did she think of him as her father, he wondered—was she, indeed, capable of thought? Mr B had noticed how strongly Pavlova reacted to different fruits and vegetables, making Farooq's lists almost superfluous, how certain greens that he did not recognise and assumed to be as dull as cabbage, occasionally took her fancy more than an apple or a bunch of grapes—but this he had assumed to be a matter, not of thought, but of instinctive knowledge inherited from her ancestors. On the other hand, seeing how relaxed she had become, how trusting with him, whatever the circumstances, he began to wonder if the human race has underestimated the intelligence of donkeys, and concluded that they are by no means the fools that we suppose them to be.

They ate in the streets that day, for there were delicious things to be had from stalls. Pavlova tried aubergines, tomatoes and slices of the big green water-melons that inside are bright red and crunchy; when they met a vendor selling ayran, a delicious cooling drink of yoghurt and water, she drank a bucketful; and when her nostrils caught the whiff of roast chestnuts or roast corn-on-the-cob she tugged against her collar and led Mr B to the stalls to indulge in what could easily have become an excess of gluttony. Their stomachs comfortably full, they spent the evening in a tea-garden where Mr B calculated from his precious map that in reaching Isfahan they were more than half way across Persia—that they had indeed travelled some seven hundred miles since crossing the border; to this he added the nine hundred miles from Peshawar to Zahedan, making sixteen hundred miles in all. Not bad, he thought, in eleven days, three of which, if not actual days of rest, had involved no travelling. But then he tried to calculate how far he still was from London and at once his brain stumbled into a ravelling cat's cradle of miles, kilometres and confusion. 'Damn!' said Mr B, out loud, and 'Damn!' again, 'How wonderful it would be to live in a world without arithmetic.' With such an outburst Pavlova woke from her snooze, and a startled waiter brought him tea.

CHAPTER 6

Pavlova is Carried on Carpets to Tabriz

WHEN, EARLY for his eight o'clock appointment, Mr B turned the corner into the street that led to Reza's shop, he was in a ready-for-anything mood, and at the next turning he became even more ebullient, for there were Reza, his son and grandsons, and a van – and what a van! This was no rusty old truck with a canvas tilt. Nor was it a battered people-carrier. This was a big, comfortable Mercedes van, painted and polished in rich claret (that is the colour of good red wine

from Bordeaux), with Reza's name and address in discreet gold lettering low on its flanks. Inside there were three seats abreast in the front, air-conditioning and a radio. Reza's son, who was introduced as Rustum (an heroic Persian warrior, the subject of an epic poem written a thousand years ago), was to drive; Mr B was to make himself comfortable in the front with Pavlova either between them or behind with the boys, reclining on the heaped carpets. The boys wanted her with them where they could stroke her back and tickle her tummy, and that, on condition that they would shout 'Stop!' at any sign of her being sick, was where she spent the rest of the day.

Rustum had driven to Tabriz many times before and they swept very fast across the fertile cotton-growing country that surrounds Isfahan, through fields of wheat and barley and the rice-producing paddy-fields of Lenjan, to the west of the city where every cottage grows its own tobacco. As that part of the province of Isfahan sits at five thousand feet or so the morning air is temperate and, driving north with the sun behind them as the day wore on, there was no need to run the air-conditioning. This is luxury, thought Mr B, wishing that he could drive all the way to England in such comfort—yet at the same time hoping that Rustum might turn off the radio and its shrieking mish-mash of Persian traditional and contemporary western music (which he hated even more than he hated arithmetic).

When they reached the outskirts of Tehran, today's capital of Persia, Rustum bore to the left, roughly westward towards Tabriz, and drove into the sinking sun. Not a great deal further, near Quazvin, he turned off the main road and in the first village they came to took the van into the yard of what in England would have been a country pub, though Mr B thought of it as a caravanserai, a traditional overnight resting-place for travellers and stabling for their animals (it was probably in a caravanserai that Jesus Christ was born). There Rustum was welcomed as an old friend, Pavlova was stabled with some sheep with whom she was immediately at ease, and Mr B was given a room on the ground floor so that he could easily keep an eye on her. There was delicious food for dinner and really good wine to drink, and musicians played haunting music to which the two boys began to dance until joined in the ring by a dozen other boys and men. Then the younger son, his voice unbroken, singing as a woman might, sang an ancient and poetic love song of all but unbearable tenderness and longing. Mr B, though he did not—as with Mirzah's songs back in Zahedan—understand one word (though he understood their fundamental meaning well enough), found this music so beautiful that he was moved to tears. There he was, in the half darkness of a moonlit night, with his arms around Pavlova's neck and tears surreptitiously creeping down his cheeks, when he began to laugh, for into his mind had come a poem that his mother had taught him when he was far too young to understand—and a Persian poem too, translated into English,

defining Paradise as '...a loaf of bread, a glass of wine, and thou...' The 'thou' in the Persian poet's mind was a beautiful young woman, but for Mr B it was his donkey.*

Perhaps Mr B and Rustum drank a little too much wine, for neither rose early the next morning—but there was no need to hurry, for the boys had fed Pavlova and taken her for a walk and they were not more than half a day's journey from Tabriz. Nevertheless, Mr B was anxious, for Tabriz was really the end of his big and comforting map and he did not quite know how best to cross the border into Turkey. He had been to Turkey many times, for he was interested in her ancient history long before the Turks invaded from the east, when three thousand years ago she was partly Persian and partly Greek, and a thousand years later was part of the Roman Empire. In the west he had swum to

* Mr B was almost as bad at recalling poetry as he was at arithmetic. His misremembered lines are from Edward Fitzgerald's translation of The Rubaiyat of Omar Khayyam (1859–1879), a thousand-year-old reflection on the full enjoyment of life. The quoted lines should read as follows:

> 'Here with a loaf of bread beneath the bough.
>
> A flask of wine, a book of verse — and Thou
>
> Beside me singing in the wilderness —
>
> And wilderness is Paradise enow.'

look at ruined cities drowned by the rising levels of the Aegean and Mediterranean Seas, and in the east he had climbed mountains to find other ruins on the borders of Russia, Armenia, Persia and Iraq, and been very badly bitten by mosquitoes. He even spoke a little conversational Turkish (a difficult language) though very badly—badly enough to make Turks laugh, which could be a good thing, for if a Turk laughs *at* you he will very quickly laugh *with* you, and then he is on your side.

If Mr B thought that in Turkey his journey would be much easier, he was both right and wrong, almost seriously wrong. In Tabriz he was still almost a hundred miles from the border and Rustum suggested that he had best make for Maku, a small town in the extreme north-western tip of Persia, and then take local transport by dolmuş (usually a battered people-carrier plying for hire like a taxi) to Doğubayazıt, the first Turkish town beyond the border. 'It is the main road from Tehran to Istanbul and the border guards are on the look-out for more important smugglers than peasants crammed together in a dolmuş.' Leaving his sons to unload the van, Rustum walked with Mr B to the bus station, where he explained to the driver of a bus to Maku that it was not only Mr B who wished to travel there, but Pavlova too. Was the driver's burst of laughter a good sign? Good, thought Mr B at first, but when he described what he would do to the donkey were she to have what Rustum translated as an 'accident' (though the driver's Persian slang had been much less polite) he was no longer quite so sure. Rustum and the driver agreed with much pantomime that Mr B must be quite mad–though Mr B himself grasped not a word of this debate–and then settled for much the same arrangements as agreed by Mirzah days earlier with the bus driver in Zahedan.

They reached Maku late in the afternoon and almost at once Mr B spied a dolmuş bound for Doğubayazıt hovering at the bus station–a really battered old station wagon covered in dust, with Turkish number plates. The driver agreed to carry Pavlova, but only in the very back where, of course, Mr B felt compelled to be with her, consoling himself with the thoughts that once over the border only twelve miles away he might change into a more agreeable dolmuş, and that, were Pavlova to be sick, this time he would be ready to catch the vomit in her hat. An old man with a crate of chickens then climbed in, an old woman with a half-grown goat, both also on their way to Doğubayazıt; and when, at last a young man clambered into the front seat, tucking a lamb under his feet, off they drove, rather gingerly, towards the setting sun.

CHAPTER 7

Mr B is Arrested at
the Turkish border

IT WAS STILL LIGHT when they reached the
border—light enough for the guard to see
that Mr B was not just another sallow Turkish peasant taking an animal to market, but
an Englishman pink with too much sun. He
waved the car off the road, opened the back
door so suddenly that Mr B almost tumbled to
the ground, and demanded his passport. Then,
with the most grim of expressions on his face
(and a grim Turk can be terrible to behold), he
disappeared into the ugly concrete bunker that
served as the border post. Damn, said Mr B to
himself, if only I hadn't been in such a hurry
to move on, if only I had waited until dark he
might not have noticed that I'm not a Turk, if
only, if only, if only… And the driver too, now
looking particularly glum, was muttering if only—if only he had compelled Mr B to sit with
the old man and his chickens or the old woman and her goat, if only he had refused to carry his donkey, if only he had been travelling

from Doğubayazıt to Maku instead of Maku to Doğubayazıt…And glum he might well be, for when the guard returned he ordered them all to get out of the car and stand against the wall as though he and his passengers were about to be shot. It was then that the guard separated Mr B from the others and showed him a sheet of paper on which there was a blurred image that Mr B recognised as himself.

Mr B did not have time to read the words accompanying his photograph, for the guard at once (and none too politely) made it clear that he was being arrested and imprisoned in the border post. To the very hour it was fourteen days since he had rescued Pavlova and brought her half way home (half way?—no, no, this was not time to dabble in arithmetic) and he was determined not to lose her now. He protested that she must stay with him and, if necessary, be arrested too, pleading that she was as much his property as the knapsack on his back. This Turk, however, was not the least amused by Mr B's schoolboyish attempt to speak conversational Turkish and, angered by his prisoner's resistance when he tried to wrest his hand from Pavlova's collar, he bellowed for help. Other guards came running, seized Mr B by the arms and, when he resisted, one thumped the breath out of him with the butt of his rifle against his chest. At this the other passengers, recognising that this was Mr B's problem, not theirs, quietly got back into the dolmuş, taking Pavlova with them, and the driver, pointing at her, shouted 'Hotel Kent, Doğubayazıt' and drove away, his rear tyres throwing up a cloud of dust in his anxiety.

Now 'Hotel Kent' were the words that, in these circumstances, Mr B most wished to hear, not because Kent in this context had anything to do with the English county that is nearest to France, but because Kent is the Turkish word for fort, and Hotel Kents are as common in Turkish towns and villages as Castle Hotels are in England. It was, moreover, where Mr B had stayed some years earlier when he and a friend had climbed the nearby mountain that everyone knows as Mount Ararat. There is just a chance, thought Mr B, that if the driver told the tale of his arrest, the owner might remember him for his eccentricities and take proper care of Pavlova.

Mr B was not long in the cell—which is just as well, for it was dark, hot, airless and smelled, as prison cells tend to in this part of the world, like an uncared-for lavatory. But telephone calls had to be made, and this was a time when long-distance calls had to be booked with operators, always took hours to achieve (and sometimes days), and more often than not were disconnected almost before they began, with no conversation taking place but a dozen telephonists between Doğubayazıt and Istanbul screaming blue murder at each other.

He endured his imprisonment for no more than four hours (though in telling the tale he sometimes extended it to as many days). At ten or so he was hauled out by the scruff of his neck, handcuffed, pushed into the back of a jeep and driven off into the night. 'Where are we going?' he asked the soldier sitting beside him. 'To the Deputy-Governor in Doğubayazıt,' was the reply. As they bounced along the rough road at high speed Mr B thought of poor Pavlova and hoped that the dolmuş driver had driven her more sedately and not made her sick. Not sick himself, but battered and bruised by the jeep, which seemed to have neither springs in its suspension nor a cushion on its seat, Mr B was desperately uncomfortable, for handcuffed he could hold on to nothing–and if that was not bad enough, clouds of dust poured in through the jeep's open sides where there were no sidescreens. At last the thirty miles to Doğubayazıt were done and Mr B was bundled into the office of the Deputy-Governor, a spacious high-ceilinged room panelled with dark reddish wood highly-polished, with, at the far end, the largest desk he had ever seen. And there, still handcuffed, he stood between two soldiers until the Deputy-Governor entered through a door behind the desk.

A tall man, handsome in a Turkish way – black eyes, black hair, black eyebrows and moustache, fine white teeth and an imperial nose – the Deputy-Governor strode forward, speaking English, his hand outstretched, but Mr B, handcuffed, could not shake it. The Deputy-Governor tut-tutted at what he appeared to think the appalling abuse of a distinguished visitor, and the handcuffs were removed, the guards dismissed with a gesture to the far end of the room. Then he pressed a bell in the panelling that Mr B could see was labelled Çay, and at once the door behind the desk opened to admit a boy bearing a tray of tea. At this point it is worth observing that all over the Near and Middle East presidents and professors, philosophers and politicians, begin their careers as scurrying boys with glasses of tea, who watch, wait, listen and learn how the world works, and then make it work for them.

At last the Deputy-Governor and Mr B settled into comfortable chairs before and aft the desk—though Mr B could not help but notice that he, the shorter man, was in a lower seat, and the much taller man loomed above him, looking down. 'Why have I been arrested?' asked Mr B a little too aggressively. 'Oh, come, come—that was not an arrest. Your government, assuring us that you are not a terrorist but some kind of scholar gipsy, has asked us to look out for you. It seems that you are walking home from Pakistan—but if that is true, then you have walked either very fast or in Seven League Boots.' Pleased with his reference to the footwear of giants in western fairytales, he smiled and continued, 'But, of course, you should have flown home on a magic carpet. We were not expecting you so soon if you were really on foot.'

Mr B at once remembered young Dominic's parting hug in Peshawar and his whispered 'I'll tell the Foreign Office.' In London he had indeed informed it and, long familiar with the aberrations of capricious English travellers, it had instructed English diplomats in Pakistan, Persia and Turkey to keep their eyes and ears open for news of an addlepated crackbrain walking westward with a donkey, particularly at border crossings. No one, not even Mrs B, was really worried about him, for he was an experienced traveller on his own, and not even the story of the donkey had raised much of an eyebrow in Whitehall, but there is always a sense of unease when a British citizen is missing and no one has a clear idea of where he might be. This anxiety, however, when translated into Turkish, had been so exaggerated that the hapless border guard (who was almost illiterate) had not unreasonably assumed that Mr B was some sort of villain, even if not a terrorist.

'But I couldn't travel on foot,' said Mr B, 'the donkey is too young, her bones not fully formed, and she could not possibly walk the twenty miles a day that I might manage easily...' And then he told the story of the evening in Peshawar and its consequences. 'My goodness,' said the Deputy-Governor, who had learned his English while training to be an army officer with English cadets at Sandhurst, 'You must go at once to the Hotel Kent—indeed I will take you myself in my jeep.' His jeep was no ordinary American jeep in drab khaki, but a British Land Rover painted an extraordinary shimmering blue as though the paint had been made of crushed pearls and peacock feathers, and it had velvet upholstery to match. The Deputy-Governor drove at breakneck speed to the hotel and sounded a fierce blast on all four horns (of which three were a special addition) when they arrived so that everyone came running. Within seconds Pavlova was brought and when she saw Mr B, like a dog she scampered to his side and adopted her usual stance of leaning against him. 'I thought it must be you,' said the innkeeper, 'I've kept a room for you.'

'Well, well…' said the Deputy-Governor, dismissing Mr B's plaint that he had not changed his clothes for two days, nor washed and shaved, and that he smelled faintly like a Turkish public lavatory, 'I must take you at once to have dinner in the best restaurant in Doğubayazıt,' adding wryly, 'as there are only two in the whole town this only means that one is not quite as bad as the other. No one else will have washed. You will not be noticed.'

'I shall be glad,' said the Deputy-Governor, delicately probing an onion that had been roasted whole in its skin, as is the way in Turkey—and delicately because, if one holds the onion too firmly with the fork, the edible inner flesh, scalding hot, may shoot from the dry skin like a bullet from a gun and plop onto the next table or hit another diner on the back of his neck—'I shall be glad if you will stay in Doğubayazıt for a day or two, for I must ask the British ambassador what he wishes me to do with you.' 'That's fine,' said Mr B, 'I'd be glad of a break from travelling and I have promised to show Pavlova Mount Ararat.' At this point the Deputy-Governor raised one of his splendid eyebrows, thinking Mr B quite mad, but he was far too polite to say so.

Now Doğubayazıt is a dusty and dirty little town in which almost every building is the colour of mud, brown mud, red mud, yellow mud and even a blackish mud that smelled quite evil before it was dried and baked into bricks. If ever a town stood on a crossroad, Doğubayazıt does, the main road lying east-west and the other north-south, and traffic thunders through it in all these directions kicking up dust that makes it look muddier still—especially when rain falls, as occasionally it does in spring and autumn; in the winter it is always under deep snow that, when cleared from the roads, is also the colour of mud. No one would go there were it not for two things of great beauty that are nearby, Mount Ararat and a ruined building that embodies all that is romantic, poetic, mysterious and beautiful in the culture of the Middle East,

the serai (or palace) of one Ishak (Isaac), the local Pasha, grown extravagantly rich on the taxes he charged on all the traffic passing the crossroads of Doğubayazıt. Time has not been kind to it; its many roofs have fallen and the local peasantry have plundered it for hearth-stones and doorsteps, but Mr B swore that its ghosts were still in residence – and that is what he told young Pavlova when he roused her for breakfast the next morning. 'But first,' he said, 'we must go and see Mount Ararat.'

They did not have to walk far to get a good view of the mountain. They walked away from the main roads where storks were nesting in the telegraph poles – great untidy jumbles of twigs and straw, in the lower levels of which hordes of sparrows were nesting too, so that

they functioned like apartment blocks with the silent storks occupying every penthouse and the noisy sparrows chattering below. In England centuries ago we drove away the storks, but in Turkey they are protected by the villagers' belief that they bring babies to the family (in England this survives as what we call an old wives' tale); Turks also believe that the younger storks feed their aged parents when they are no longer able to care for themselves.

Soon there was nothing between them and Mount Ararat several miles away, and they were walking across meadows of tall grass and wild flowers with the beautiful mountain seeming to float ahead of them, not craggy like Mount Everest or Mont Blanc, but almost human in its silhouette, as though a beautiful naked woman had fallen asleep on her back and slept so long that she had turned to stone. They made slow progress, for Pavlova had never seen a meadow before and to her sensitive nose it smelled so sweet and fresh and warm that she could not stop nibbling. Mr B too was overcome, but with nostalgia, for he was old enough to remember that before the Second World War such meadows were everywhere in England, bright with the reds of poppies, the blues of scabious and cornflower, and the yellows, pinks and half-colours of a hundred other flowers. When they found a patch of shade they closed the great umbrella, sat and rested, and with his arm about Pavlova's neck Mr B told her the story of the Flood. Now you too may want to raise an eyebrow, just as the Deputy-Governor did, but Mr B had always had dogs (and the occasional cat) at home, and he firmly believed that they understood every word he said to them, reinforced perhaps by the ancient belief (now all but forgotten) that between nightfall on Christmas Eve and dawn on Christmas Day all animals can speak, and do, but we are never awake to hear what it is that they say. He did not believe that they spoke English or any other human language, but was convinced that not only do they comprehend meaning but they pick up human thoughts that are never expressed in words.

This may well be true, but the tale of Noah and his Ark was a little too complicated for Pavlova, and while Mr B recalled as best he could this great event early in the very first book of the Bible, she quietly munched every daisy within reach. 'Imagine,' said Mr B, 'a God so angry with His first attempt at creating decent men and women that He decided to destroy them all in a great flood, and then to start again. He decided to destroy all the animals too, but, relenting when He saw that Noah was just such a decent man as all men should be, He ordered him to build a great ship into which he must load two of every creature, with food enough for all, and ride the terrible storm of rain that would last forty days and forty nights and drown the earth. Noah did as he was asked, and when the earth began to dry, beached his ark on the mountain we call Ararat. And that, dear Pavlova, is why you and I are here, for you are a descendant of the two donkeys in the ark, and Noah was my grandfather a thousand greats ago.' That said they opened the umbrella and wandered back to Doğubayazıt.

There was a message for Mr B from the Deputy-Governor, and an invitation to dine with him again. This Mr B was glad enough to do for he had found him a most agreeable companion. Before his training as a soldier at Sandhurst, he had been educated at the London School of Economics, yet in spite of this had a civilised cultural background very like that of Mr B. They shared an interest in opera, a very European entertainment, and even in ballet (which was why he was so much amused at encountering a donkey answering to the name of Pavlova). He spoke fluent French and German as well as English, and he was Deputy-Governor of Ağri, the province in which Doğubayazıt lay, because he could also speak the Persian and Russian that were sometimes diplomatically needed in disputes over borders with Ağri's immediate neighbours.

'You,' he said to Mr B, looking him straight in the eye (but with a hint of twinkle), 'could so easily have been in serious trouble at the border. And you are being a nuisance to the British ambassador. He has asked me to detain you for another day or two while he sends a van to collect you. You will note that it is a van, not a splendid embassy car, that is coming – this is because he knows of the donkey. He thinks you are mad and a damned nuisance that he can do without, but is anxious to help. In the van you will be driven all the way to Istanbul, where you will be a guest in his villa on the Bosporus. If you take Pavlova to Ishak Pasha's palace tomorrow that will occupy the day (you may have my jeep), and you will probably set off for Istanbul the following morning.'

'Whoopee!' said Mr B who, having never quite grown up, quite often used old-fashioned schoolboy slang. To tell the truth, he was dreading yet more of this journey, more explanations, more arrangements, more anxiety. 'Whoopee!' he said, vaguely remembering that Turkey is at least a thousand miles from end to end by road and rail.

CHAPTER 8

The British Ambassador
Sends for Mr B

WHEN THE VAN ARRIVED Mr B was delighted. It was much the same, he thought, as the splendid Mercedes van in which Rustum had driven him from Isfahan to Tabriz – indeed it was the same, but Mr B was not much interested in vans and could not tell one marque from another. This van differed in that it was black and had black windows all round through which to see but not be seen, and on its doors a handsome crest, discreetly small, had been painted, making it quite clear that this van was unlike all others in that it belonged to Her Majesty the Queen of England. The driver, whose name was Osman, had removed the passenger seats and converted the space into a mobile stable, its floor deep in straw, fitted with two big containers with lids that could be removed when the van was stationary – one full of food fit for a young donkey, the other carrying her drinking water. This Osman had done so that Pavlova could, if necessary, safely be left in the van overnight.

Osman, short, dark, strong, middle-aged, very capable and speaking excellent English, though he had never been to England, had decided that this part of the journey should be a pleasure for his passenger, not just a job for himself, and though he had driven the most direct route from the embassy in Ankara (the capital of Turkey), he did not intend to drive straight back there and then on to Istanbul. 'We shall go to Van,' he said, 'where there is a thousand year-old church – quite wonderful – on an island in the lake. And there are cats that swim for pleasure and catch fish; their fur is white and they all have one eye that is blue and one that is green.' Mr B had not the heart to say that he knew the city of Van very well (he had even, years before, bought a pair of carpets there), and the extraordinary Armenian church on the island of Aghtamar, and that he even had a friend at home in Wimbledon who had two white Van cats with eyes in green and blue, though he had never seen them swim – so he kept quiet about these things and about all the other wonderful churches (ruined, of course) that he had seen in the far north-east of Turkey in the provinces of Kars and Artvin.

And so it was that Pavlova, in a little ferry-boat, sailed to the island from the southern shore of Lake Van, through a cloud of sparkling blue dragonflies, and walked round the church (and, since no one objected, even in it), and then up the hill behind it to the towering cliff on which sea birds nest, though it is two hundred miles from the Black Sea in the north, and three hundred from the blue Mediterranean Sea in the west. Mr B was delighted to see that, as on the walk to Mount Ararat, Pavlova needed no collar and lead, but, just like a dog, when she stopped to examine a trace of some other animal (even bees – by whom she was discreetly fascinated and never risked a sting), or to try her taste buds with yet another flower, she then broke into a scamper to catch up with him. She is more like a dog every day, he said to himself. And Osman fell for her – 'We have a donkey at home; she lives in a stable and my mother rides her to market, but she shows no interest in anything.' 'In that case,' said Mr B, 'when you return home you must talk to her, take her for walks, feed her by hand – then she will begin to know you and become your friend.'

So began what really was a holiday for Mr B. He did not have to worry about the next stage in the journey, about walking for miles, or bouncing about in a truck, or finding somewhere to sleep, or carrying food and water, and most of all he did not have to worry about looking after Pavlova, for she was very comfortable in her mobile stable and had been quick to learn that if, for any reason, she was separated from Mr B, she would very soon be reunited with him. Osman drove them through villages so wretched that the villagers collected heaps of drying dung for winter fuel, past water buffalos wallowing in muddy ditches, past strings of camels and wandering peasants with big black tents of canvas with sides of straw woven into matting that could be rolled up to keep them cool. And when they reached a town or city he seemed always to know where to find a quiet and comfortable hotel, a restaurant where the food was really good (though Mr B had developed a taste for baked onions), and a safe place to park the van and Pavlova overnight.

Never once did Osman let Mr B pay a bill, and always, on arrival, he said something sotto voce (that means very quietly, but not quite so quietly as a whisper) to the man in charge (in Turkey it is almost always a man, occasionally a boy, but never a woman) that resulted in the immediate obsequiousness of too wide a smile and too enthusiastic a welcome. To Mr B, who all his life and everywhere would like to have been invisible, all this was tiresome, even objectionable, but he had to admit that it resulted in quiet rooms with the best views and very good dinners indeed. Nevertheless, he suspected (though he had no evidence) that Osman might be doing deals over the bills and pocketing a percentage for himself. There was also the problem of the public events of which Osman seemed always to know; to his dying day Mr B was to remember an interminable evening in Diyarbakir, one of the oldest and noblest cities in eastern Turkey, having to sit in the front row at a national festival with the President of the Turkish Folk Dancing Society. All the dances, all the howling and yowling seemed to Mr B to be the same, and a giant amplifier just behind crippled him with cramps because he had to sit for hours with a finger stuck in his left ear.

Some two hundred miles west of Diyarbakir, in the mid-afternoon of a very hot day, they drove into Kahraman Maraş, a city famous for a kind of ice cream that is unique to Turkey. Like elastic, it can be stretched between hands a yard apart, bundled together in a lump and stretched again – and again and again – a party trick for those who sell it, though it tastes much the same as any good European ice cream (it was in Turkey, by the way, that the sorbet, the fruit-flavoured water ice, was invented). In a café it is best eaten with a knife and fork, for to a spoon it clings and plays its stretching trick, and can make a frightful mess. Osman stopped the van outside the most splendid of the many cafés in the main street, and when Mr B stood gasping at all the sweetmeats in the window, his jaw dropping lower and lower, a waiter came out with something delicious between his finger and thumb and popped it into Mr B's mouth. It tasted of honey and nuts, bacon and eggs, pastry and marmalade, all at the same time, and Mr B went in, sat down and ate much more of it, and other sweetmeats, and ice cream, and sorbet crushed into a frappé, and black, black coffee. Then it was Pavlova's turn. Osman lifted her onto the pavement, Mr B pulled her ears through the holes in her hat, and the waiter stretched elastic ice cream under her nose so that she could first lick and then bite it. Mr B swore that she shut her eyes and murmured a long 'Mmmmmmmmm...' in ecstasy. People took photographs.

The road north from Kahraman Maraş has, by Turkish standards, a good surface and runs through mountains with many twists and turns that tempted Osman to drive as though at the wheel of a racing car, and he was thoroughly enjoying himself when poor Pavlova was sick—very sick—and when they stopped to let her walk a little and recover, she continued to be sick, heaving and choking, though her tummy was by then long empty. Mr B vowed that he would never again give her rich and sugary things to eat—at least, never in such quantity—and tried to give her carrots to clean her teeth, but she refused and hung her head. Osman, meanwhile, had kicked out onto the side of the road most of the straw that was her bedding, for the wind to blow away. To replace it was a matter of urgency, so they set off at a sedate pace with Pavlova between them in the front, her head lolling on Mr B's lap again, just as it had during the very first part of the journey from Peshawar—and it occurred to Mr B that she was now markedly bigger and heavier.

They found more than straw. They found a farmhouse in which they could spend the night, have dinner, and stable Pavlova with other donkeys—much bigger, shaggier animals, who greeted her most tenderly. Dining with the family meant sitting on the floor round an enormous circular tray heaped with rice, roast peppers, tomatoes, potatoes and pieces of stewed mutton still attached to chunks of bone that appeared to have been chopped by a blind man with an axe.

'Today,' said Osman the next morning, aware that Mr B's mood was fidgety and that he wanted to move on, 'we shall drive three hundred miles and get beyond Ankara, and then, with luck, tomorrow we shall be in Istanbul by early afternoon and I shall deliver you to the Ambassador.' This meant that they were to make a mad dash across Cappadocia (pronounced Kapadokia in Turkey), an area right in the middle of the country where the wild and weird volcanic landscape has eroded into sandy rocks that resemble gigantic ant-heaps. For centuries the local people hollowed caves in them in which to live, and when Christianity was established two thousand years ago, it became a place for monks and hermits to live, hollowing tiny churches in the soft rock and then painting them with stories from the Bible. Mr B knew it well, for Alexander the Great had been there, his troop marching southward in the broad valley of the River Halys (now the Kizilirmak), while he himself and a few friends impetuously galloped fast over the flat salt lake to the west.

Mr B heaved a sigh of relief (though without appearing to do so). He would, in the absence of Pavlova, have been happy to revisit Cappadocia and surprise old friends, but she was not absent, she was there, at his side, and entirely his responsibility. He had, so far, been extremely fortunate, but three weeks on the road had worn him down. This was not a holiday; nor was it one of his gypsy scholar expeditions – as his long walk in the footsteps of Alexander the Great had been; this was a rescue mission and, if anything went wrong, it could be a disaster for poor Pavlova. And added to this disquieting sense of unease was another that he had not felt before – the call of home, his dogs, his books and his carpets. So on they sped but even clever Osman could not avoid the dense traffic that is drawn to Ankara – just as it is drawn to London, Tokyo and New York – and as he was very tired they stayed where they easily could and made the best of it.

In those days the road from Ankara to Istanbul was one of the most dangerous in Turkey and Osman chose to drive with great care; even so, when they stopped for lunch in a dust-bowl of a town from which they could just see the Sea of Marmora (which means Sea of Marble – but there is precious little marble left) they were within an hour of Istanbul and in even less of a hurry. Thus, when a group of Turkish wrestlers gathered in the garden of their restaurant, to Oman's evident delight, Mr B thought it would be churlish were he to say that they could not stay and watch (at least, he thought, there is no music). Now Turkish wrestling is not like English or Olympic wrestling. For the most part it takes place in the open air on a patch of grass (if one can be found); the wrestlers are barefoot and naked to the waist, but wear trousers of very stout black leather, held up by a belt or coil of rope that can be grabbed and held by opponents. Slippery with olive oil from top to toe, the wrestlers struggle for a firm grip and the contests can be very funny (though not intentionally so); there may be rules, but of these

Mr B was unaware and Osman, if he knew them, made no attempt to explain. Both were taken by surprise when, after a particularly long bout, the triumphant wrestler seized poor Pavlova (still wearing her straw hat) and, holding her above his head, performed a victory dance that, had it been with a lion or a leopard cub, would have looked magnificent, but with an adolescent donkey in a hat was hilariously funny. She slithered against his torso when he put her down and, returning to Mr B covered in oil, soaked his shirt and trousers with it too. Poor Mr B had no clean clothes into which he could change, but Pavlova was taken to the kitchen quarters of the restaurant, where she did not greatly care for being sluiced in cold water and getting soap bubbles up her nose.

CHAPTER 9

In Stanbul the Ambassador's Wife Takes Command

A T PRECISELY 2:15 IN THE AFTERNOON of the twenty-third day of their acquaintance, Mr B and Pavlova were driven by Osman across the first great bridge in Istanbul to connect the continents of Europe and Asia, and on along the European coast of the Bosporus to the summer house of the British Ambassador. There they parted with hugs, for Osman had grown fond of both Mr B and Pavlova—and Mr B's enormous tip now made him fonder still.

Poor Mr B had last worn a clean shirt and trousers when dining with the Deputy-Governor a thousand miles away, and had since spilled honey and ice cream on them, to which Pavlova had added a most generous smudge of oil. He was in no fit state to meet the Ambassador—but the Ambassador was not yet at home and it was his wife, Laetitia, who greeted Mr B. She, fortunately, was quite accustomed to dealing with scruffy English travellers who had for no good reason chosen to climb the mountains of Hakkari in the far south-east, or to steer a canoe along the fast-flowing Euphrates (Turkey's—and Europe's too—most history-laden river), or to follow the footsteps of Alexander the Great, and was well prepared for as many Mr Bs as might turn up; she also knew a great deal about horses (as, probably, all women called Laetitia do) and was as much prepared for Pavlova. From the size of his knapsack she judged that Mr B was carrying not much more than a toothbrush and a book or two, and summoned a servant. 'This is Haydar,' she said, 'he will see that your clothes are laundered and, meanwhile, find others for you from my husband's wardrobe. This evening is informal but…' and as her voice tailed off Mr B finished the sentence for her with 'But I am a disgrace.' She laughed. 'We shall be friends. Now who is this?' turning to Pavlova.

Mr B then told her the tale of that early evening in Peshawar and all its consequences, and when he reached the point where Osman drove like a racing driver and Pavlova was sick, she called Haydar to ask if Osman had yet left for Ankara. He had not, and she asked that the fresh straw be transferred from the van to provide bedding in a pretty little gazebo in which Pavlova was to spend the night. Then, while Mr B showered and tried to find something among the Ambassador's old clothes that he could wear without looking like a clown (the Ambassador was a much larger and more imposing man), Laetitia took Pavlova in hand and curried her coat so expertly that she was as pretty and sleek as a whippet.

A plot was forming in Laetitia's mind, and when the Ambassador (whose name was Horatio) arrived with other guests and all were in the shaded garden with glasses in their hands, and Mr B had told the tale of Pavlova a second time, Laetitia said to her husband, 'Darling, you won't mind, will you, that I have asked Osman to stay on a day or two with the van?' To this Horatio said neither yes nor no, but, squinting at her over the rim of his glass, replied, 'You have something in mind?' 'Well yes. As we've brought Mr B and Pavlova all the way from Doğubayazıt, we can't just dump them on the roadside here and let them thumb a lift to Greece. Why don't we tell Osman to drive them to the border? Then we shall know that we have done our best and that on your territory we could have done no more. And I would like to see them on their way.'

Laetitia took it that Horatio had agreed (as, indeed, he had, though he had uttered not a word) and with some unnoticed signal summoned servants, first to light the garden with candle-lamps, and then to bring a delicious supper of cold dishes to nibble in the heat, as is the Turkish way. At this, Pavlova, who had been gently investigating the flower beds and shrubbery, trotted to Laetitia's side and would have licked her plate had a sharp tap on the nose with fingers dipped in gin not deterred her; her response to it was a funny little four-footed jump that Mr B had not seen before. One or two of the guests were slightly disapproving and shooed her away, but others thought it

wonderful that a donkey should behave like a family dog.

The following day, wearing his own clothes freshly washed and pressed, Mr B was early down to breakfast—not the bread and honey to which he had become accustomed as the only Turkish breakfast, but English bacon and sausages flown from London. Hurrah for Fortnum

and Mason, thought Mr B as he crunched the crisped rashers and succulent bangers, the oldest, grandest and prettiest of grocers' shops in the whole wide world, suppliers of provisions to the Duke of Wellington in his battles with Napoleon and to Florence Nightingale in the Crimean War; have they any idea how exotic their sausages and bacon seem in far off Istanbul? Laetitia too was early. They made the oddest pair, for Mr B's clothes were evidently very old and unfit even for a charity shop, while Laetitia, in immaculate white linen, carrying an enormous floppy hat in the most expensive straw, seemed to have stepped from an international fashion magazine. Horatio waved them off with the wry smile of a man not quite certain what his wife will do next, and Osman took the van on to the road along the north coast of the Sea of Marmora that leads to the border with Greece.

Now the Greeks do not much care for the Turks, and nor do the Turks much care for the Greeks – there has been too much disagreeable history between them over the past five hundred years, a history of occupation, religious conflict, cultural suppression, rebellion, revolution, freedom, war, suspicion and mistrust. The border between them is only eighty or so miles long, but there is such hostility and cussedness at the main crossing points that travellers of every nationality can be delayed for two hours and much more. It was Laetitia's intention, however, not to be delayed for as much as two minutes, for she had decided not to offload Mr B at the border post of Ipsala, but at Alexandrupolis, the first substantial town beyond. It was Osman's careful inclination to join the queue and wait, but Laetitia urged him to drive confidently on and only stop if guards ordered them to do so. One did, but Laetitia waved diplomatic papers at him and pointed to the van's diplomatic plates and coat-of-arms, and suitably cowed he let them pass without even thinking to ask what might be behind the black windows through which he could not see.

'Why did you do that?' asked Mr B, who had been preparing to dismount. Laetitia answered that he and Pavlova stood very little chance of a lift if they attempted to hitch-hike in Greece and that they might well find themselves tumbled into a ditch several times a day. 'Instead, in Alexandrupolis I shall put you both on a train to Thessaloniki, which is a big, busy, bustling, filthy town where neither you nor Pavlova will be able to breathe, so polluted is the air, and at that point you must fend for yourselves – but I shall have the satisfaction of knowing that I have got you safely through nine-tenths of your journey across Greece.'

Mr B thanked her in the quiet way that some Englishmen have when a great kindness has been performed – too quiet, some may say, but to Mr B this was an occasion when words are not enough and, therefore, the fewer used the better. He would, he knew, find some deeper way of thanking her when back in England. 'One small thing puzzles me,' he said. 'Why are you so beautifully dressed? You are smuggling a donkey over the border, yet you wear white linen fit for a garden party at Buck House.'*And for the second time on this long journey, 'Wait and see' was the reply.

He had to wait until they reached the railway station at Alexandrupolis, and then he saw how composed and seductive the wife of a British Ambassador can be. Mr B could speak hardly more than a word or two of modern Greek, but Laetitia seemed to have absolute command of the language. She put on her splendid hat while Mr B and Osman unloaded Pavlova and

* Slang for Buckingham Palace.

fitted her saddlebags; she then led them into the booking office. He watched her speak
to the booking clerk behind his little window;
he watched her being swept through a door
marked Station Master; he watched her come
out again with papers of different colours in
her hand. These, she explained, entitled him
to travel, with Pavlova, in the guard's van, all
the way to Thessaloniki, but he might have to
change trains two or three times—hence the
several sheets of paper. Mr B, she had persuaded them, was a scholar of great renown in England, and must be made comfortable; the Station Master had therefore agreed to load his
very own office armchair (in which he was accustomed to doze every afternoon) into the
guard's van, and with any change of trains this
chair would accompany Mr B as far as Thessaloniki. And with a brief cuddle for Pavlova, a
hug and a kiss on the lips for Mr B (a special fa-
vour) and a whispered, 'Now you know why I
dressed as I did,' she stepped into the blackness
of the van and Osman drove her away.

CHAPTER 10

The Slow Train of Andreas Papagos

AS THEIR TRAIN WAS LEAVING in half an hour Mr B and Pavlova went shopping for their supper. With fruit and vegetables for her, bread and cheese for him, and lots and lots of water for them both, they returned to find the armchair being loaded – a hefty wooden frame with padded back and arms (from which, very worn, some cotton wool and horse hair were escaping), and a deep seat made deeper by the exhaustion of the springs (the Station Master was a heavy man). Mr B shook hands with the guard, lifted Pavlova and climbed aboard. The track was winding and the train very slow. Night fell; Pavlova was asleep on her sheepskin and Mr B dozing in the chair when the guard announced that they must change trains. The new train was not scheduled to depart until morning, but the new guard, a friendly old man with white whiskers whose name was Andreas Papagos, said that, as they had brought the chair, they should make themselves comfortable in his van and spend the night there.

Andreas was so old that he had never been to school, but had always, even as a child, worked on the railway—that he spoke English was entirely due to his passion for American films,

particularly westerns, and Mr B was occasionally to be surprised by his vocabulary. He should have retired long ago, but everything that there was to know about the line from Alexandrupolis to Thessaloniki, he knew, and he knew the travellers too, from every town and village, every peasant, every herdsman (his van was often full of sheep and goats), everyone who had anything to take to market. As the train trundled along at what often seemed not much more than walking pace, he told Mr B how the Greeks in this part of their country had in the past hundred years fought wars against the Turks (who had occupied the whole of Greece for five full centuries), against the Bulgarians (who would have liked to occupy it), against the Italians and Germans (who invaded it in World War II), and even against themselves in a terrible civil war between the Communists and their right-wing opponents, between Republicans and the supporters of a Royal Family that had repeatedly been expelled. He had, himself, as a boy before his whiskers grew, cut the throat of a Bulgarian in 1913.

Mr B was mightily entertained by all this but, looking at Mr Papagos now, great-grandfather to eighteen children of throat-cutting age, kindly, gentle and considerate (he had brought a battered white enamel jug of scalding coffee, bread straight from the oven, and a sweet melon for Pavlova), he found it difficult to reconcile this sweet old man with the image of a bloodthirsty boy that he painted of himself. But then, thought Mr B, I am not recognisable as the schoolboy that I was at fifteen, nor even the young man of twenty-five or thirty-five; we all change, and we go on changing till we die.

While Mr B was ruminating thus, Mr Papagos was thinking too, worrying about what this odd pair of passengers would do in Thessaloniki, where they would find too many pedestrians on every pavement, too many cars on every road and, worst of all, no obvious way on foot out of the city and on to the road north to the border with Macedonia and the rest of Europe, with scarcely a word of Greek in which to ask. Even if Mr B found the road twenty miles away from the city centre (an exhausting journey for Pavlova), it would be a motorway on which no speeding driver would stop. Were he Mr B, he'd prefer to join the road after the Macedonian border, about fifty miles north of Thessaloniki, where the motorway is reduced to a very dangerous, but ordinary, two-lane road. If, therefore, Mr B and Pavlova left the train at the village of Doirani, within a mile or two of the border, they could get a lift across it and on to this road that all traffic must take if northbound through the newly independent countries of what used to be called Yugoslavia – or even Jugoslavia.

'I have been thinking,' said Mr Papagos. 'So have I,' said Mr B, who had indeed been fretting, for he knew this road and Thessaloniki, having driven it many times on his way to Turkey. 'Shall we see if we have been thinking the same things?' he asked – and, of course, they discovered that they had. Mr Papagos revealed his plan to put them off at Doirani, where there is a camping-site on the lake just the other side of the border. 'With luck, you and Pavlova will simply walk there and spend the night. And with more luck, some camper there – perhaps a German (it is crowded with Germans) – will give you a lift tomorrow morning.' Then he gave Mr B a slip of paper with the address of an old friend who, should they have difficulty at the border, might find some private way of crossing it.

At Doirani the train stopped and Pavlova and Mr B stepped down onto the track; so too did Mr Papagos, and gravely they shook hands, both men feeling that they had known each other for years, yet knowing in their bones that they would not meet again. The train chugged away to the south and Mr B, opening his umbrella against the fierce sun, stood, his eyes fixed on it as it grew smaller and smaller until he could see nothing more than the faintly moving blob of shabby red paint that was the guard's van. He wondered if, perhaps, it might be the oldest van of all vans on Greek railways, even the oldest in Europe, for under the chipped and faded paint its ancient timbers showed signs, not just of wear and tear, but of war and revolution, for there was evidence of shrapnel damage and in an idle moment he had begun to count the bullet holes, giving up when he reached thirty-two and, interrupted, felt disinclined to start again. Had it started life as a Turkish van on what was then a Turkish railway? Had it, briefly, been Bulgarian? Had it carried soldiers to the front in the Balkan Wars of 1912 and 1913? Had it carried the British troops known as the Gardeners of Salonika in the Great War of 1914–18? Had Italian and German troops used it to reach the not unfriendly border of Turkey when they invaded Greece in World War II? And so on. For some long moments, triggered by the old van, Mr B's imagination had transported him through a hundred years of history.

Both Pavlova and Mr B were glad to be on their feet again and their pace through the little town was jaunty, but in the heat very few people were about, and when they reached the border post not one single guard or soldier was to be seen. On tiptoe so as not to attract attention from anyone not asleep within the concrete block-houses, Mr B and Pavlova crossed into Macedonia, the birth country of Mr B's great hero, Alexander. At the camp-site he hired a little cabin for the night in which both he and Pavlova could sleep, and then went to the lake and paddled. Pavlova had, of course, never had so much water under her nose, and she clearly loved cooling her hooves in it,

and then her knees, and, suddenly, feeling the first cool splashes on her tummy, she began to splash deliberately. People came to the bank to watch and children begged to ride her, but Mr B said that she was still too young to car-ry passengers – 'Next year, perhaps,' he said, and then wondered how many children would next year demand to spend their holidays be-side Lake Doirani because the English donkey might be there.

Pavlova splashing was exactly the advertisement that Mr B needed, and within an hour every camper knew that they were walking all the way to London unless someone offered them a lift. And someone did. He was a German with the kind of vehicle that is part car and part truck, with a four-door cabin for passengers and an open flat-bed back in which tent and sleeping-bags and barbecues may be piled high. What he really wanted was to buy Pavlova for his children but, no matter how hard he pleaded and how much money was offered, Mr B refused – and it was because of the honest obstinacy of his refusal that Mr Helmut Riemenschneider offered him a lift. 'We have another week here,' he said, 'and if I take you to the main road tomorrow my kids will have forgotten Pavlova by the time we go home. Let's go early in the morning, before they are awake.' And thus it was that by eight o'clock Mr B and Pavlova were standing by the main road, the E75 indeed, with heavy traffic thundering past. Helmut had dropped them eight miles short of the next village to the north, so that they had only that distance to walk if no one stopped for them, and they could reach help of some kind before the blazing heat of day made walking difficult and dangerous.

CHAPTER 11

On Foot until Rescued by a Rolls-Royce

NO ONE AND NOTHING STOPPED. A few cars slowed so that passengers could laugh at the idea of a man and a donkey thumbing a lift, and many lorries sounded their horns, though whether as a safety warning or a hoot of mockery, Mr B could not decide. He grew tired of constantly looking over his shoulder and developed a crick in his neck, and Pavlova, occasionally stumbling, began to look as though she was not enjoying herself. They reached the next village in great despondency and there Mr B had two ideas. The first was to desert the E75 and take to much smaller roads, quieter, slower, safer, but likely to result in lifts only over very short distances; but for this he would need a very good map, for roads in the Balkans rarely end in the direction first suggested, and many just fade into the landscape half way up a mountain or nowhere in particular. His second idea was to find someone in the village who could make a simple sign on a pole that he could easily carry over his shoulder—and it was this he chose to do, though without realising that he could not, at the same time, carry the umbrella.

He found what he thought might be a post office (it was not) and explained what he wanted. The shopkeeper did not understand him, and he did not understand the shopkeeper. They went next door to the blacksmith, who did, after a fashion, understand, but thought that Mr B wanted the sign in wrought iron, which would have been absurdly heavy. Then all three, and Pavlova, went to the village carpenter and he understood at once, measured Mr B for the length of the pole and the height at which it was to be carried; and set about constructing it. By late afternoon it was ready: it weighed a little less than Mr B's umbrella and carried only one word on the signboard—LONDON—two feet across, in Roman capitals, in black on white, with a neat little decorated edge, also in black. The blacksmith then inspected Pavlova's hooves and trimmed them a little to be even, offered her hay and stabling for the night, and to Mr B he offered a straw mattress on which to sleep in the shelter of his smithy, on the fire of which he casseroled a stew. Mr B could not see what went into the stew, he knew only that the stew already existed and that the blacksmith added great handfuls of something to it, his hands anything but clean; he hoped it was chopped lamb or mutton; he feared that it might be one of Pavlova's distant relatives. Bearing two large bottles of home-made slivovitz (the very strong plum brandy of the Balkans), the carpenter joined them to make a merry feast. Pavlova was the only one of them not to have a headache in the morning.

Soon after eight next morning Mr B and Pavlova were back on the main road, she carrying a bale of hay that was a parting present from the blacksmith, he the signpost over his shoulder with the one word LONDON clearly visible to all traffic coming from behind. Still no one stopped. Glossy Mercedes after Mercedes roared past, BMW after BMW, all with the letter D for Deutschland on their number plates. There

were dilapidated old cars from Croatia and Macedonia, Hungary and Herzegovina, Bosnia and Bulgaria, and shiny well cared for cars from the Netherlands and Belgium, even Denmark, but not a single car with a GB plate. They trudged on until Mr B knew that very soon he would have to open his big umbrella to give them a scrap of shade, and if he carried that over their heads, he could not display the sign and keep a hand on Pavlova's collar.

He was on the point of despair when he heard the sound of a car with a broken exhaust behind him; this was not a reason to look back and he did not, but the sound interested him, for as a schoolboy trapped in the room in which bespectacled masters with a cruel streak attempted to teach him double periods of mathematics, he had relieved his boredom by closing his eyes, listening to the exhaust note of passing cars and guessing what their engines were. He could not multiply fifty-three by seventeen or divide it by two and a half, but he could distinguish an engine of four cylinders from one of six, a straight-eight from a v8, and the vertical twin of an old Morgan from the flat-four of a Jowett Javelin*–until now an utterly

* An advanced & ingenious car that ceased production in 1954.

useless accomplishment. Now, he said to himself, screwing his eyes tight shut, this sounds like a really big v8, and unscrewed them to see that the car already speeding into the distance was an early Rolls-Royce Silver Shadow with a GB plate, shabby in faded maroon and long unwashed.

The words then used by Mr B are quite unprintable, for in polite society they are said only in *extremis* or in literary conversation by fashionable novelists. He and Pavlova trudged on. Then he heard the sound again, but from the north, and the Rolls-Royce reappeared, but travelling southward really fast, making an appalling racket. 'Not a good Rolls-Royce,' said Mr B to Pavlova as it swept past them, 'in fact the worst they ever made—Silver Shadow, they called it, and that is exactly what it was, the shadow of a noble firm's former self, the plaything of plumbers and spivs. Had it stopped, I think we should not have got into it.' But then Mr B heard the exhaust again, lower this time, a burble rather than a bellow, and knew that the car was behind them, slowing down; just past them, it stopped, and the driver, lowering the window, said the magic words—'Want a lift? I was going too fast with a Mercedes just behind me the first time I went past.'

'I have a donkey,' said Mr B. 'So I saw,' said the driver, 'that is my main reason for returning. I don't much care for the human race, but a donkey in trouble is a different matter. She can get in the back and lie on the seat.' 'But what about the upholstery?' Mr B enquired—to which the driver uttered one of the words beloved of modern novelists. Some rearrangement of luggage was performed, the gap between the front and back seats filled and covered with Pavlova's sheepskin, and then Mr B and the driver introduced themselves. He was a bibliophile—that is a lover of books and all things bookish, a collector of rare editions, illustrations and manuscripts, but he was also (and more often) a bibliopole—which is an almost forgotten term for a bookseller. His first name was Hector, his surname one of those triple-barrelled combinations of three ancient names that suggest a thousand years of history that must not be forgotten—though it is of scant interest to anyone but themselves that one of the three families fought for Harold at the Battle of Hastings, the second fought for William the Conqueror, and the third descended from the wrong side of the bedclothes when

Charles II was on the throne.

Hector, it seems, had been book hunting in Athens, having been given a tip about the recent death of a miserly Greek bibliophile, and had in the boot of the car some manuscript volumes that he suspected should never have been allowed to leave Greece, so important were they. 'Mostly letters,' he said, 'of interest to anyone concerned with the history of Crete, but with two absolute stunners – from Titian, the grand old painter in Venice, to El Greco,* the tyro in Crete, suggesting that he should come to Venice and join his studio.' 'Gosh!' said Mr B, the only possible response to the discovery of such important documents (at least important in the history of art), astonished that they should have lain undiscovered since the middle of the sixteenth century. Hector was, therefore, making for home as quickly as possible, but the blown exhaust was, unfortunately, drawing attention to him. He had had the Rolls-Royce for some years – the second-hand successor to other Rolls-Royces, all of which, on the advice of an uncle, he had neglected and,

---

* TITIAN (c.1485–1576), the leading painter of his day in Venice. EL GRECO (1541–1614), born in Crete, then a Venetian possession.

as they say, driven into the ground – 'the cheapest form of motoring,' the uncle said, 'and a Rolls-Royce that is battered, scratched, scraped and never washed is not a car to attract the notice of a thief, though other drivers will notice and give way.' Hector reckoned that he held the speed record for rounding Hyde Park Corner.

'I suspect,' said Mr B, 'that your silencer has a hole in it, that it will take no more than half an hour to repair – and that most of that time will be spent waiting for it to cool before the work can be done.' 'What do you know about it?' asked Hector, a little aggressively. 'Oh in the days when I used often to drive to Turkey, the exhaust was always the first thing to cause trouble and I learned to carry a kit with which do roadside repairs.' 'I can't imagine you under a car,' said Hector. 'Why not?' said Mr B. 'Just because you find me travelling with a donkey, do you take me for a fool? We don't even need a garage – a blacksmith can do the job, and if you can bear to go to the village where I spent the night, I know exactly where there is one.' And so back they went and were rapturously greeted by the blacksmith, who had never worked on a Rolls-Royce and was now thrilled to do so. The shopkeeper and the carpenter came to see him working on the car, and so did half the villagers;

and Hector took photographs that, later, suitably enlarged in England, he sent to the grinning gap-toothed blacksmith to hang in his smithy as a souvenir of the event. Mr B was both right and wrong about the half hour—the blacksmith took fewer than five minutes to weld a patch on the exhaust, but the greetings, the celebrations, the slivovitz and the farewells took the best part of two hours. And then, switching on the engine, it was as quiet as a Rolls-Royce should be, and all that Mr B could hear was the whispered burbling of an idling v8.

Hector drove on, and on, and on till nightfall, well on the way to Belgrade, to an hotel that he had found comfortable on his outward journey. He asked for two rooms, but there was a hitch – the hotel did not accommodate donkeys and had no outbuilding in which Pavlova could be stabled. 'In that case,' said Hector, 'you must let me have three rooms' – but this was a ploy that the obdurate receptionist simply could not understand, even as a joke. He rang a bell and someone more important appeared to whom Mr B assumed that he said, 'Here we have two crazy Englishmen and a donkey. They wish to book two rooms for themselves and a third for their little friend. They look as though they might be difficult.' This more important man smiled the unctuous smile that he was accustomed to adopt when having to deal with the eccentricities of travelling Englishmen to whom he did not intend to give way, but then he recognised Hector and the smile changed abruptly to one of unalloyed welcome – 'Ah, you were here a week ago' – as he recalled that this was a guest who had eaten well in the dining room, and had drunk even better. He should not, he thought, turn away two such Englishmen because they had a donkey as well as a Rolls-Royce. 'Of course we shall find somewhere for the donkey – not a room with a view, perhaps,' he quipped, 'but certainly a room in which she will be safe and comfortable.' What he had in mind was the room in which slept the kitchen boy, Gavrilo, the wretched boy who peeled potatoes, washed the pots and pans and was always first up in the morning to set the kettles boiling. His room opened directly into the yard at the back, so that Pavlova could go out if she wished, and it contained nothing but his bed, for Gavrilo was an orphan and, at fourteen, possessed nothing but the hand-me-down clothes in which he lived and worked and slept—not even one paperback book that Pavlova might try to eat. Straw was scattered on the floor, the hay that was the blacksmith's present was brought in and a big bucket of water set down in the corner. Mr B bade her good night and went upstairs to have dinner with Hector.

And what a merry dinner the two men made of it, though almost everything on the menu could be translated as meatballs with this and that (always true in Serbia, the country in which they now were, notorious for its dismal and drab cuisine). They drank a bottle of white wine with the first course, of red with the second, and more slivovitz with the third, Hector very much in command and claiming a Scottish grandfather on his mother's side as the reason for his ability to swallow so much alcohol with no obvious sign of any serious effect. Poor

Mr B did what was expected of him but, when Hector was not looking, surreptitiously emptied his glass into the vase of dying flowers on their table. Not surprised to wake in the middle of the night in need of water, he thought to clear his fuddled head by wandering downstairs to see if all was well with Pavlova—and found the prettiest sight he'd ever seen: there, in a rectangle of light shafting through the window, was Pavlova on Gavrilo's bed, her hooves hanging over the edge of it, with the boy lying beside her, his arm about her neck. Both were fast asleep. Neither stirred.

In the morning, after breakfast, Mr B sought out the kitchen boy, thanked him for looking after Pavlova (Gavrilo did not understand a word, but recognised the sense) and pressed, because he had no Serbian money, an English ten pound note into his hand. Gavrilo, who had never had so large a sum of money, nor felt a note so crisp and clean between his finger and thumb, flung his arms round Pavlova's neck for the last time, kissed her on the nose and shook Mr B's hand. They waved goodbye as the Rolls-Royce engine sprang into life, but as soon as the car was on the move, the hotel manager, who had observed their farewells, sidled up to Gavrilo and deftly snatched the note. In doing so, he planted a seed of hatred in the boy's mind that was, a decade or so later, to bear a terrible fruit—but that's another story.

CHAPTER 12

A Night in a Monastery

WOULD YOU MIND if we don't go very far today?' said Hector after a few miles. 'There's a monastery in Croatia, more or less on the way, that has a famous library and I'd rather like to browse there for a while if they will let me in. I have an illuminated manuscript at home that is a bit of a puzzle, and I think it may be from this part of Europe. I've brought some photographs just in case.' 'No, not at all,' Mr B replied, 'I'm perfectly happy to browse myself, provided that Pavlova is happy too...'

And Pavlova was happy, for the monastery had a stable—in which, alas, there were no longer any horses (nor even a donkey)—and a shaded garden surrounded by a cloister in which she could safely be allowed to roam. Best of all, two of the old monks, who could recall a time when the stables of Saint Florian were still in use, decided to exercise their old equine skills and prepare her as though she were being entered for a competition. Tenderly they

washed and dried her; tenderly they brushed and combed her; and when they had finished, her coat was again as soft and fine and silken as that of any whippet, gleaming in the sun.

Meanwhile, Hector and Mr B were entertained by the Abbot, a man of great scholarship who was happy to show them the monastery's library, but who would not leave them alone in it. 'You must forgive me,' he said, 'but I have, in the past, left visitors alone to browse, and been sadly surprised to find how easily they succumbed to the temptation, not only to put books in their pockets, but tuck larger volumes into their shirts. Where books are concerned it seems that no man is honest; we have lost many to university professors, museum curators, other librarians, and to passing politicians who have no intellectual interest in what they steal, but steal because they can. I now write to almost every visitor to say that this or that has not been returned to its proper shelf, and if he (and it is always he) has by chance gathered it up with his coat (a coat over the arm is so often the camouflage for the theft) or other things, we shall be very grateful for its return. This almost always works, but if it doesn't, then I inform the relevant ambassador.' 'We are without coats,' said Hector, 'without evil intention, and our camouflage, Pavlova, is in your stable.' 'You must stay for lunch,' replied the Abbot.

It was a frugal lunch – a hard-boiled egg each and some salted anchovy fillets, a salad of rather bitter leaves that Mr B thought even Pavlova would not relish, bread without butter, very hard dry cheese, water and a white wine so thin that even Hector could not stomach it: coffee did not follow. Such monkish fare was nevertheless enough to fortify them for more hours in the library at the Abbot's invitation – he had warmed to them when, over lunch, Mr B had told the tale of Pavlova's rescue. And when they had had their fill of books and manuscripts the Abbot asked, 'Where had you planned to spend the night?' – and to their vague response followed with 'Then you must spend it here.' This, Hector and Mr B felt it would be churlish to refuse, though, as both had in their time spent other nights in monasteries, neither was enthusiastically looking forward to it. They were shown to stark rooms with beds and very little else in them, and bidden to come down to dinner in the refectory at seven. Bathing was to be done in ice-cold water. Mr B spent an intervening hour in the cloistered garden with Pavlova for company, and then saw her put to bed in the stable, all alone, but with clean straw on which to sleep, water, her hay and all sorts of fruit and vegetables to eat, all grown by the monks.

After so light a lunch they were hoping for a more substantial dinner – not oysters and roast beef, but at least grilled carp from the monastery carp-pond (all monasteries once kept carp in ponds so that they should never be without fish on Fridays); imagine, then, their disappointment when more hard-boiled eggs were passed in a basket from monk to monk, more fillets of anchovy in bowls of salted oil, with boiled potatoes the only luxury with the main course, and grapes (fresh from the vine and warmed by the afternoon sun) to enliven the now even drier bread and brick-hard cheese.

The wine, however, was a rich red to the eye and full-bodied to the tongue, and the simple deliciousness of the anchovies warmed by hot potatoes that were soaked in olive oil was a gastronomic discovery to both Englishmen. They slept well enough on it, and though they would not have been surprised that breakfast too consisted of eggs and anchovies, it did not — only with bread hot from the oven and honey from the monastery hives were they set up for the day.

'I know,' said Hector, as they drove away from the monastery — where he and Mr B had given a donation far larger than the bill they might have paid in an hotel with hot water and fine

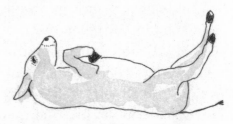

food, and two old and tearful monks had embraced Pavlova as she prepared to be helped into the car — 'that you are anxious to get home to London, but if, when we eventually reach the motorway, we turn away from it on to the minor roads, we shall drive through a landscape so beautiful that we should take time to enjoy it. It is through such a mountain landscape that young Albrecht Dürer must have walked for weeks on his way south to Venice to study with Giovanni Bellini five centuries ago, and imagine Peter Bruegel walking from the Netherlands to Rome to talk to Michelangelo, seeing mountains for the first time.†* Just think – you might have trodden in their footsteps if you had indeed walked all the way from Peshawar.' Mr B looked at the map and saw how winding the mountain road would be and tried to count the hairpin bends. 'Pavlova might be sick,' he said. 'Then I shall resist my impulse to throw the car round all the bends – just two or three, perhaps – and we shall stop every so often to take her for a walk.'

To other motorists on this neglected route – and there were very few – the sight of a battered Rolls-Royce and two men sharing with a donkey the shade of an umbrella must have seemed

---

* DÜRER (1471–1528), a great German painter from Nuremberg who sought instruction from Bellini in Venice.

BELLINI (c.1431–1516), Titian's predecessor as the most influential painter in Venice.

BRUEGEL (c.1524–1569), the most inventive and adventurous of Netherlandish painters in his day.

MICHELANGELO (1475–1564), the towering genius of painting, sculpture and architecture in the High Renaissance.

an amusing delusion as they raced past in their Alfa-Romeos, taking the hairpin bends as fast as they dared. Hector kept his promise and stopped the car wherever the road was wide enough for Pavlova to walk, and Mr B was later to swear that she had looked at the mountains, the valleys and the vast distances quite as intently as he, seeming to store images in her mind. Though occasionally distracted by a plant or shrub that might be good to eat, or tempted to taste the trickle of a spring breaking through the rock-face, she did what she always did when Mr B stood still—pressed against his hip and looked in precisely the same direction. 'We can still sense the ghosts of history here,' said Mr B with a slight shudder, as though the temperature had dropped—and what was even odder was that Pavlova, at precisely the same moment, uttered a low whinny, as though discomforted; the only sound that Mr B had heard from her before was her braying at the border guard on the day that they entered Persia.

'We are,' said Hector late in the afternoon, 'about eight hundred miles from home. How would you like to spend the night here in the middle of nowhere, get up very early and drive to London in a day?' 'That,' replied Mr B, 'requires you, at the very least, to drive at eighty miles an hour for ten hours without stopping for petrol, food, drink or little walks for Pavlova—and even at that speed you must add time for crossing the Channel. The last time a Rolls-Royce established such a record was probably in 1910 and it's a bit late to establish another. And I think you've under-estimated the distance. It makes better sense to plod on until nightfall, join the Autobahn to Munich, press on and spend the night in Ulm or thereabouts—and even at Munich we still have some seven hundred miles to go. And there's another point—for Pavlova's sake I'd like to reach home in daylight.'

At this Hector uttered a wild cry, a sort of 'Yippee' or 'Wa'hae' or 'Home, James, and don't spare the horses,' and stamped hard on the accelerator. Once across the German border they stopped to fill the car's almost empty tank and munch on succulent hot sausages and coffee, for Hector and Mr B had eaten only some of Pavlova's store of fruit since their breakfast of bread and honey (Hector had also eaten some of her vegetables, peeled with his pocket knife, but these had made him belch most horribly). Thus fortified, Hector drove the big car as fast as it would go, and then, folding back the wing mirrors, made it go a little faster—well over a hundred miles an hour. He was, of course, showing off, for (like most men) he had never quite grown up and was in his boyish element as, with Beethoven symphonies blasting from the radio, the car swept past Munich and Augsburg and even Ulm, two hundred miles away. Mr B, who knew these historic cities well, would have liked to show them to Pavlova, but did not pursue the thought for it was now almost as though he was being beckoned by his comfortable house, his garden, his dogs, his books and even by Mrs B, as though he could hear the owls and foxes that hunted in his garden by night, and taste his breakfast porridge and the oysters he enjoyed so much; had he been a small furry animal with whiskers, he would have twitched them in anticipation. Hector too felt the nearness of home as he urged his old car to overtake a thousand glossy upstarts before sweeping past Stuttgart and into Karlsruhe, a pleasant city on the River Rhine.

It is a strange phenomenon, this gathering intensity of the call from home the nearer one draws to it. In Pakistan Mr B had felt no homesickness, nor in Persia, nor in familiar Turkey; the demand for a quickening of pace had not begun until he was in Greece, and now, north of the Alps, his longing to be home was becoming almost painful. Hector too, in Athens discovering his precious manuscripts, had not a single thought of home, and since meeting Mr B had positively lazed his way towards the north until quite suddenly, when dropping down from the Alps and that much nearer England, he too felt the pull and wanted to race home.

'Where are we?' asked Mr B, who had been snoozing since Ulm but had wakened in response to the slower speed at which the car was ambling through darkened streets. 'Karlsruhe,' said Hector, 'I know a decent little hotel here with an underground garage in which Pavlova will be quite safe. We'll take her for a walk and refill her bucket, but we have no option but to leave her in the car overnight.' And so they did, in the deepest, darkest part of the garage, where she was least likely to be disturbed, with the windows slightly lowered. It was the first time that Mr B had left her utterly alone and out of earshot, but by now she knew from experience as early as the yard in Zahedan and as recently as the monastery stable, that he always returned. While his footsteps were still audible she fell asleep.

A hundred feet away, Hector and Mr B gulped a bottle of Piesporter (a fine German wine) and what food the hotel had to offer so late in the evening. *Rippchen mit Kraut*, a peasant dish of ribs of pork with Sauerkraut, was quickly re-heated and put before them, followed by *Käse mit Musik*, which is to be translated as 'Cheese with Music'; this, another peasant dish, of hard cheese long matured in olive oil, eaten with raw sliced onions, is so indigestible that the human stomach immediately provides the music, one way or the other. This is a German joke. Both men, exhausted by a day that had begun with breakfast in a monastery and ended with a drive as thrilling as the Monte Carlo Rally or the Mille Miglia, did not stay awake long enough to hear it.

CHAPTER 13

How to Smuggle a Donkey Over the Channel

HECTOR WAS DRIVING DUE WEST to pick up the French motorway system when he said, 'We have a problem.' 'Something wrong with the car?' said Mr B, who had not paid much attention to anything other than Pavlova since returning to the Rolls-Royce. 'No, no. It is Pavlova. We have no idea what the rules and regulations may be covering the import of a donkey into England. Were she a dog we would have to have certificates proving that she is not carrying rabies, and even with the necessary papers she would be taken into quarantine for six months.'

'But she's not a dog.' 'Exactly. And we don't know what to do.'

'Racehorses come into the country every day, race and go out again.'

'Pavlova is not a racehorse, and she intends to stay.'

'What do you think we should do?'

'Well I don't think we can risk attempting to

drive through Customs with her sitting on the back seat for everyone to see, but, if she is out of sight, we can, if asked, say that we have nothing to declare, because we haven't – not a drop of wine, not a single cigarette. And if the car is searched and Pavlova is found, we can honestly say that we did not know that importing a donkey is contrary to regulations. If it is illegal and she is found, she will be taken from you whether or not you declare that you have a donkey in the car.'

'But if she is not on the back seat, where can she be, and what is to prevent her from braying at a hostile Customs Officer – just as she did with the border guard in Zahedan – and giving the game away?'

'Sleeping pill,' said Hector. 'When we are about half an hour from Calais and the boat we shall stop and rearrange things and give Pavlova the pill. With your front seat back as far as it will go there should be room for her, and when she's a bit wobbly we'll put her on the floor under your legs, which will act as camouflage. There you can keep an eye on her, check her breathing and soothe her if she wakes – which may be possible, for we should risk only half a pill. I take two and she must be much less than half my weight.'

'Bit risky,' said Mr B, appalled at the thought that he might lose her.

'Well what's the alternative? A fishing-boat unloading you below the White Cliffs of Dover?'

Mr B grudgingly agreed. To lose Pavlova to a curious Customs Officer would be unbearable, but would half a pill be enough, or a whole pill far too much, and would there really be room enough in the front—'She can't curl up like a dog, you know, her back has to be straight.'

It seemed that no sooner had they crossed the French border than they were on a side road leading nowhere in search of food for Pavlova—for that is what Hector said—but this was no nowhere, this led so immediately to an enormous supermarket that Mr B suspected that Hector had been there before. Indeed he had, and when he went in he made a beeline for cheeses, sausages and hams that were of no possible interest to Pavlova, and then he moved on in search of tinned duck swimming in duck fat, again a peasant food, yet at the same time a delicacy so rich and so un-English that it is irresistible. Mr B, rather half-heartedly, for Pavlova still had vegetables given her by the monks and even half the bale of hay, found young carrots still with their leaves for her, and some crisp white turnips with a purple flush, and then he too bought cheeses and mysterious misshapen sausages that looked as though they had been buried and exhumed, or at the very least left to moulder forgotten in a farmer's larder, for he bought such things on the principle that the more disgusting the appearance of a sausage, the more delicious it will prove to be. Then he joined Hector, emptying the shelf of every tin of duck, so many indeed that the wheels of their trolleys could hardly turn under their weight and had to be dragged, squeaking and groaning, to the car. When they loaded their contents into the boot the hefty old car sat back on its haunches and heaved a great sigh.

One purchase that they did not load directly into the car (though indirectly they did most certainly) was a custard tart. This Mr B had seen on the patisserie counter, the last before the check-out desks, and it had, it seemed to him, spoken of all the custard tarts he had ever eaten when travelling in France, and particularly of one in Paris when he was a student and had not the money to pay for such a luxury, but bought it nevertheless instead of lunch. There it lay, thirty centimetres in diameter, the delicate pale yellow of a wintry sun, a thing of egg yolks, milk, sugar and vanilla, encased in pastry of the most delicate crumbling quality, not the thick stodge to which, in England, we are accustomed. Bought and paid for, five minutes later, astonished and not altogether agreeable French housewives in the car park were to see it given to Pavlova. As if it were not enough to see Mr B and Hector gently lift her from the car—and no ordinary car, but a Rolls-Royce (imagine the rolling of the two Rs when, later, they spoke of it to their husbands)—they had then witnessed the breaking of this by no means inexpensive delicacy into manageable parts and, from the flats of their hands, fed to a donkey—'imagine it, ten whole francs down the throat of a donkey!'

Unaware of their hostility, Mr B was once again convinced that Pavlova had murmured a long 'Mmmmmmm...' of contentment, well aware that she had had a special treat. Mr B gave her a carrot or two to clean her teeth.

Then they sped on again, past Metz and Verdun, where French and German armies fought a terrible battle of attrition in 1916, half way through the Great War in which both their fathers had, as very young men, fought. Then they drove past Rheims, its almost ruined cathedral a noble, romantic and melancholy monument to that same war, and on past the great hill on which stands the very strange and beautiful cathedral of Laon (ignored by too many travellers), visible for miles. Both men, in their youth soldiers themselves, preoccupied by so much heavy-hearted history, were silenced by it, and even when Mr B saw a beautiful heron, not by a lake or pool but foraging for shrews or voles in a meadow by the noisy motorway, he said nothing of it.

To the north of Arras Hector pulled off the road into an *aire*, the French word for a small flat space (even for the contact face of a hammer), but in this context not so small, but a wooded retreat sheltered from the motorway and the hum of its traffic. Here they exercised and fed

Pavlova and, deciding on impulse to give her a whole sleeping pill, Hector cut into a sweet apple with his pocket knife, pushed in the pill and plugged the hole. She swallowed it after a single crunch. They waited anxiously, watching for the first wobble, and when they saw it Mr B, tucking one arm around her bottom and the other round her chest, attempted to lift her into the space in the footwell of the front seat. She was still a tiny donkey but in the month since that night in Peshawar she had grown; Mr B had occasionally noticed that she was heavier and a little more of a burden to lift, but not that she had grown taller and longer – and now she did not, could not, would not fit in the space that they had planned. Her long legs did not quite fold enough, her head was at an awkward angle, and her bottom was where Hector's feet should be. They imagined having an accident and explaining to the French police that it had happened because a donkey's bottom was stuck under the brake pedal – and then decided that she must travel on the floor between the front and back seats. They pushed the front seats forward until Mr B's knees were under his nose and Hector was hunched over the steering wheel – and still she did not fit. Then Hector cleverly unscrewed something and the front passenger seat came off its runners, making just enough space for Pavlova if Mr B sat in the back, arching his legs over her to hold the loose seat jammed against the dashboard. Hector then threw Pavlova's blanket over him with the instruction that he must pretend to be unwell, even an invalid too ill to speak, being rushed home to consult his London doctor, while Hector would see to all the business of tickets, reservations and so on.

They were in luck. They did not get lost (as so many drivers do) on their way to the harbour in Calais, and even though they were within twenty minutes of the departure of a ferry, Hector was persuasive and the car was allowed on—the very last. With a recording of a great French opera, *Samson and Delilah*, wafting from the open windows of the Rolls-Royce to seduce any French officials who might be inclined to be disagreeable, Hector drove past them to the ramp, was beckoned up it, and the car neatly tucked into the last corner behind an enormous lorry, almost hidden in the gloom. Of all this, Pavlova was oblivious.

They were, of course, compelled to leave her and climb to an upper deck. Mr B spread his outstretched fingers on her ribcage and was reassured to feel her breathing evenly, and he made sure that nothing could cover her nose while they were away, but to lull his unformed fears for her was quite impossible. Upstairs they lunched – thought it was more of a picnic than a proper lunch, and a French picnic too, for this was a French boat – and on a sea that seemed to have not a single crested wave on it, they ate crusty French bread and salty French butter (which tastes entirely different from English butter), a delicious duck pâté, an even more scrumptious sausage sliced very thin (flavour is always enhanced when the slices are as transparent as lace curtains and can lie on the tongue instead of immediately being chewed), and two cheeses – one of goat's milk, perhaps a week or so too young, the other blue-veined, dry, subtle and so exquisite that Mr B was determined to remember it, but his notebook was down in the car and he forgot. Having forgotten, he was to waste hours in London cheese shops, searching, searching, until he became notorious; eventually he found another blue cheese, though from Italy, that appealed to him as much, obliterating the by then faint memory.

He was also to search even more purposefully for Persian tiles so that he could recreate for himself the tiled bathroom that had so delighted him in Zahedan, but though he found in antique shops a handful that did not belong together, and made a nuisance of himself in Christie's, the great auction house in London where one might reasonably expect to find whole panels of tiles from time to time, he never did. Instead, bathing every day in a bathroom so ordinary that it could have been installed in any house anywhere in England in the second half of the twentieth century, he thought every day of Zahedan and in his memory the tiles became ever more beautiful in colour and design, impossibly beautiful indeed, and because, eventually, they existed only in his mind's eye, they could never have been matched. It was just as well that he had bought those carpets from Reza in Isfahan, for had he not, he might well, over a period of years, have romanced them into things so wonderful that no such carpets could ever have existed. Instead, he was to reach home without having had a second thought about them, there to find a huge parcel that neither he nor Pavlova could have carried, with within it the carpets exactly as he remembered them, no finer and no worse, and be content.

When passengers were instructed to return to their cars Pavlova uttered not a sound nor moved her limbs. Outstretched fingers on her ribs again reassured Mr B that she was still alive, but the shouts and bumps and clangings that are so much part of disembarkation from a ship did not at all disturb her. To Hector it was almost disappointing to be waved on after the most cursory of passport checks, for having bidden Mr B play the ageing, silent invalid, he had composed for himself a web of truths, half-truths, downright lies and passionate appeals to sympathy for helpless animals that he was convinced would get Pavlova past any Customs Officer, and was excited by the thought of playing centre stage. He might, indeed, have made a rather good bad actor, but never a bad good one. Instead, it seemed that with scarcely a glance the Customs Officers were happy to get rid of this filthy old car and all that might be in it and waved it urgently on, oblivious to the fact that Hector had changed the music from French to English and that they were to be diverted from their duties by the strains of Elgar's cello concerto.

By the time they were, at a sensible pace, settled on the road from Dover, Mr B was desperately anxious. Pavlova showed no sign of waking and though her breathing was as regular as ever, he was uneasy in case Hector's sleeping pill had been too strong; she was, he thought,

still only a baby and, though a very different shape from Hector, much, much light-
er in weight. He suggested stopping and attempting to wake her. 'No, no,' said Hector, 'if
we are seen to stop on this first stretch of motorway we shall draw attention to the car, and
the police will be here in a trice. It will then
be obvious that we have smuggled a donkey into the country. Be patient until we are on the
ring road round London, for then she could
have come from anywhere. I'll hustle on, but it
would be silly to be caught exceeding the speed
limit. There is a vast motorway stop near Wes-
terham where we can, without attracting attention, chuck a bucket of water over her.'

Without attracting attention, indeed? They
did find a shaded spot but it was hardly isolated.
Pavlova was asleep as ever, and a Rolls-Royce
with its rear doors open and two men bent double with their bottoms in the air was a sight that
a curious small boy with an ice cream could not
resist. 'Go away,' said Hector. And go away he
did, but only to return with his father, just as
Pavlova showed the first signs of wakening – an
open bleary eye and a feeble scrabble with all
four legs. Mr B dipped his hand in her bucket of
water and, with dripping fingers, wet her muz-
zle – and then she made a strenuous, though

ill-coordinated, effort to get up. With Mr B lifting her head and shoulders and Hector heaving her rump, they hauled her out of the car and suddenly she was standing (albeit rather wobbly) on her delicate little hooves. Greedily she emptied her bucket and Hector took it to refill while Mr B walked her slowly up and down.

'What is it?' enquired the small boy's father, and Mr B, not wanting to engage in conversation, heard himself snap, 'A miniature donkey.' 'How much?' said the father, 'Not for sale,' Mr B replied. 'Everything has its price,' said the father, 'how about a hundred quid?' Mr B shook his head at a hundred and fifty, two hundred and two hundred and fifty, and was mightily relieved when Hector returned just as the father asked, 'Where did you get it then?' not knowing what his answer would have been. 'This is a perfectly ordinary donkey,' said Hector, 'it just happens to be the runt of its litter and very small—it is often the case that the mother, when she has six or eight babies, cannot feed them all, and then, if they survive by hand-feeding, they become miniatures. All you have to do is look at the small advertisements in *The Times* where they are two-a-penny.' All this was nonsense, not one word of it true, but the boy and his father (quite certainly not a regular reader of *The Times*) took themselves off, convinced that tomorrow they too would have their Pavlova.

'You know,' said Mr B as Hector swung the car back on to the road, 'the first thing I shall do when I get to my desk is to write to that fat television director and tell him that I'm back, with my donkey, and in a month instead of a year.'

'No you won't—you may write the letter, but I'll wager that you'll tear it up. It's not your style to crow—nothing is achieved by putting your thumb to your nose like a schoolboy (though I know you've never grown up), and are you quite sure that you are back in a month and not a little longer? A month against a year has a nice sharp edge to it, but five weeks does not.'

At this, Mr B started counting on his fingers and, of course, lost count and had to start again. Once he counted thirty-one days—but only once, his other counts were more, and one, perhaps the most scrupulous, made the total thirty-four, inconveniently more than the prized month. 'No,' he said, 'you are quite right. I should ignore that contemptible idiot. But I shall write to young Dominic, for without his intervention here in London, I might not have had such a jolly time in Doğubayazıt. That was a near thing, very nearly a disaster. I wonder for

how long I might have been kept in that concrete cell. I wonder what would have happened
to Pavlova.' And at that sudden chilling thought
he shuddered.

CHAPTER 14

Home in Wimbledon

IN THE LATE AFTERNOON they reached Mr B's house in Wimbledon. When the high wooden gates opened the dogs began to bark, and as Hector's Rolls-Royce stopped in the shade of a tall cedar tree, out they ran to welcome it – that is, two of them did, Carrington the whippet and Kahlo the brindle Staffordshire, but the old Alsatian, Kollwitz, the real guardian of the house, stood at the front door and watched. And what she saw was her beloved master stooping to return the ecstatic greetings of the younger dogs, their leaping and bounding and running in circles, and then she watched him walk towards her with the others still about his ankles, kneel and put his arms about her neck and murmur 'Kollwitz, darling girl,' the endearment that he reserved only for her. She, in return, slowly wagged her great long tail, nuzzled his ear, and then leaned against him with all her weight – just as Pavlova instinctively had done. All this, with a wry smile, was watched by Mrs B who knew from long experience that in this household the animals came first; besides, she had had a telephone call from the Ambassador in Istanbul and knew that Mr B had been last seen waiting for a train to take him across Greece—and there, she could reasonably assume, he could not be kidnapped by brigands, bandits or drug traffickers.

Mr B had always had bitches and had named most of them after poets, composers and philosophers, but his current pack were named after women painters of the twentieth century. The whippet was dubbed Dora Carrington because he considered them both to be skittish and scatterbrained, poor Kahlo after Frida Kahlo because she was the ugliest dog he had ever had (though he loved her all the more), and Kollwitz, the Alsatian who was the dog whom he loved most deeply, after Käthe (Katie), whom he held to be the greatest woman artist ever.

Eventually scrambling to his feet, his hand resting in the thick ruff of hair at her neck, he led Kollwitz to the car and introduced her to Hector (Carrington and Kahlo had already introduced themselves), in whose trousers she showed consuming interest, as though trying to solve a mystery. And then, with the 'Hey Presto!' of a conjurer, he solved it for her by opening the door and assisting Pavlova to step onto the gravel. Kahlo barked, furiously, and backed away, lowering her haunches; Carrington immediately recognised a running animal and raced away inviting her to chase; and Kollwitz, having sniffed her from nose to tail, hoisted herself on her hind legs and, with forepaws resting on Pavlova's shoulder, gently reached to lick her nose. Pavlova, who had never before encountered a dog, took all this as though she were accustomed to such a variety of greetings, and lowering her head, blew gently, but audibly, through her nostrils, greeting Kollwitz in return.

While all this was happening Hector had quietly unloaded Mr B's share of the cheeses, sausages and tins of duck, together with Pavlova's saddlebags, sheepskin and the great white umbrella, and was ready to move on, anxious to be back in Hampstead in time to have dinner with his handsome Russian wife. He embraced Pavlova, hugged Mr B and thumped him on the back, said 'See you soon,' plonked kisses on the cheeks of Mrs B, and swept off in the Rolls-Royce with a swoosh of wind and tyres, his foot unnecessarily hard down on the accelerator. And see each other soon they indeed did, and often too, for their few days of adventure together proved to be the foundation of a close and lasting friendship.

Mr B's house was built more than a hundred years ago, before the invention of the motor car. Attached to it were a stable and a coach-house large enough to accommodate a proper carriage and a pony-trap. The stable Mr B had converted into a library when in the house he had run out of space for books, but had kept the original stable door of the kind that is divided into top and bottom halves so that, with the top open, the horse can stick his head out and watch the world go by. In the coach house he kept a beautiful old Mercedes in which the dogs were not allowed, along with a lawn-mower, the garden tools, twenty-three spare typewriters collected so that he would never be without one (he was a mighty thumper on their keys and they were always breaking), pots of paint that were half used and would never be used again, some wooden shutters from a previous house and a small Honda car for the convenience of the dogs if this was ever necessary. A sensible man would have called a salvage firm to take most of this away, but Mr B was not invariably sensible, and he decided instead to move his books elsewhere and lodge Pavlova in the old stable. There she was very comfortable, for Mr B robbed one of his bedrooms of a big old and careworn settee that had occasionally served as a bed – and

on this she was as happy to sleep as on the back seat of Hector's car (to her it seemed quite logical for a donkey to sleep on furniture). On the walls he hung her kilim saddlebags and two paintings of Mount Ararat that he had painted on his first journey to eastern Turkey, so that the room looked and felt more like a cottage drawing-room than any stable. Any misgivings he may have had about her sleeping alone were swiftly quieted by Carrington who, like all whippets, craved warmth from any source, and immediately chose to sleep with Pavlova, curled up against her tummy, refusing to move when Mr B closed the stable door for the night.

For the first few days Pavlova was allowed to wander round the garden only in the company of Mr B and the dogs. It was not a formal garden; overhung by trees, crowded with shrubs and bushes, Mr B had let it run wild for the benefit of birds and insects (he was inordinately proud of its rare stag-beetle population), and among its visitors were wild ducks and herons, for it had a proper pond deep enough to drown a standing man, in which frogs, newts and exotic dragonflies multiplied every summer – and there were squirrels and foxes too. None of these had Pavlova ever seen. Here she could find apples, pears and acorns and even eat them from the trees, crop the grass and test her taste buds on sage, thyme, bay and rosemary, but there were also yew trees in this tanglewood, and to donkeys (horses too) the yew and its berries are lethally poisonous. As Mr B had planted some of these himself and had trained roses to climb in them, their destruction caused him great sadness – but down they had to come and every trace of them removed, every dead twig and fallen leaf, for what would have been the point of bringing Pavlova all the way from Peshawar only for her to die a painful death?

Carrington thought Pavlova ought to run and found her rather dull when she did not – but a donkey has to learn to run and, above all, learn how to stop rather than crash into things, and the garden was not quite big enough for that. Kollwitz, on the other hand, as grave and mag- isterial as an old Alsatian should be, enjoyed her company, and the old dog and the young donkey spent hours together, snuffling their way round the perimeter wall of the garden on daily voyages of discovery, always followed by the robins who feasted on the grubs and insects they disturbed.

Nevertheless, after long preoccupation with letters that had to be written to Farooq the phar- macist, Mirzah the poet, Rustum the carrier of carpets, the Deputy-Governor whose name he did not learn, the Ambassador in Istanbul and, particularly, Laetitia the most skilled of diplo- mats, for all of whom suitable gifts had to be most carefully chosen—for care is a thousand times more valuable than cost on such occa- sions—the day came when Mr B ventured to Wimbledon Common, a vast and wild wood ter- ritory of trees and ponds and even a little river, tamed here and there by patches of golf course and putting greens. Leaving the younger dogs behind he took only Pavlova and Kollwitz, for he had absolute trust in the common sense of the old dog, and knew that if he let go of Pavlo- va's collar and she began to run, Kollwitz would bring her back again. But Pavlova did not run;

she stayed very close, as though dismayed by so large an open space, all the time touching him with her shoulder no matter whether they were in the open stretches of the golf course, or wandering in the deep woods. In her short life she had known only pavements, roads and railway platforms, but here she was ankle-deep in dry dead leaves, or up to her knees in brambles, or a millimetre deep in turf so short and thick and velvety that her teeth could get no purchase on it; here she was expected to shoulder her way through yellow gorse, clamber over fallen tree trunks and cross streams that, though no wider than Mr B's stride, had over many years worn small chasms in the earth, too wide to leap, too steep to clamber down and up. Only when Carrington was at last allowed to join these walks did Pavlova begin to run – and it was on the golf course that it first happened, with golfers shouting 'Fore!' to begin with, but words much less polite as the whippet ran in ever wider circles with Pavlova doing her best (but failing utterly) to keep pace with her, Carrington causing utter confusion by changing tack and running full tilt under the donkey's tummy as though she were some sort of bridge. After this madcap episode Pavlova seemed to lose her fear of open spaces.

One day, when Mr B needed to do some shopping at the nearest supermarket—too little to justify taking the car, yet too much for one man to carry if he succumbed to temptation (as he almost always did)—he took her saddlebags from the hooks, fitted them over Pavlova's shoulders and set off down the hill with her. Now the hill is so steep that the architects who designed the supermarket installed a lift so that pedestrians from the street above can take a short cut and drop straight into the building. Into this lift stepped Mr B with Pavlova and pressed the DOWN button. It is a lift entirely of glass and Pavlova gazed from left to right and back again as though this was the most exciting event of her life—so much so that Mr B began to wonder if she might like to go up in a balloon, a train of thought cut short when the lift touched bottom, the doors opened, and two women waiting to get in screamed and dropped their shopping. People came running; some tutted disapprovingly and spoke of health, safety and the myriad germs with which Pavlova must have filled the lift, and Mr B struck entirely the wrong note when he said to the noisiest of these, 'But Madam, I have slept with this donkey for more than a month and caught not so much as a common cold.' Other curious spectators could hardly contain their laughter, and still others, horsey women (of whom there are enough in Wimbledon to sustain at least two riding stables), mobbed poor bemused Pavlova with oohs and aahs, and pats and strokes, and pretty bunches of young carrots.

The canny supermarket manager, sensing that if Pavlova were to be a regular visitor, children might want to come to his supermarket rather than any other, soothed the silly women with a generous fistful of vouchers and hustled Mr B outside. 'Bring the donkey as often as you want,' he said, 'but always telephone this number—it is my direct line—and a member of staff will bring you down in the lift as though Pavlova is an important guest, tether her in this shaded corner by the door and keep her company. Do you mind if people give her apples and carrots and broccoli?' The manager was quite right—Pavlova was an attraction (and not only to children), his sales of fruit and vegetables rose quite considerably even though Pavlova visited not more than once a week—indeed he reckoned that she raised the profits at his store by fully one per cent, and at Christmas sent Mr B a goose and a bottle of the very best pink champagne, a tipple that, alas, he disliked with peculiar intensity.

There were many adventures further afield in Hector's Rolls-Royce, with Pavlova on the back seat, her head resting in Olga's ample lap, and poor Mrs B squeezed between the donkey's bottom and the door, the dogs fitting in where they could, all higgledy-piggledy. They went to Beachy Head and led Pavlova almost to the edge of it to look at the windblown Channel that she had crossed but never seen, and she gazed towards France with the same intensity as she had contemplated the Alpine mountains of Carinthia. At Polesden Lacey, the nearest country house to Wimbledon, belonging to the National Trust (of which Hector was a devoted member), their visit was frustrated by the ghost of Mrs Ronald Greville, its last private owner, a very grand political hostess once described in her old age as 'a galumphing, greedy, snobbish old toad'. Hector had not expected to be allowed in the house with Pavlova and the dogs; he wanted only to walk with them in the garden, but the guardian at the gate pointed to a notice stating that no dogs were allowed. 'Very well,' said Hector, 'they will be very disappointed, but we shall leave them in the car. As there is no similar notice applying to the donkeys, only she will come with us.' There was then an argument: 'Logic dictates,' argued

Hector, 'that in the absence of such a forbidding notice, donkeys are to be admitted.' 'Not so,' said the guardian, 'there is no notice denying entrance to elephants and dinosaurs, but that does not mean that they are welcome to lunch on Mrs Greville's flowers.' How odd, thought Hector, that the odious Mrs Greville, who had died some thirty years before, should still be invoked as the proprietor of the garden. This was clearly a losing battle, so he swung the great car round and drove the mile or so to Box Hill, the high point of the North Downs, and there they spread their picnic and lay in the sun while Pavlova and the dogs rolled on their backs in the rough grass, raced and chased and joined in finishing the odds and ends, much happier than they would ever have been among

Mrs Greville's beastly herbaceous borders.

There was no such problem at Stourhead, a hundred miles west of London in deepest Wiltshire, for Hector had had the common sense to make sure that no one there would object to a donkey walking in the garden – he had, indeed, argued that donkeys had almost certainly been employed in the eighteenth century to carry picnics – and even people – to the furthest reaches of the vast Serpentine lake around which the garden was designed, and that to use a donkey now would greatly increase the charms of the garden to every modern visitor. He was, of course, quite right, and when he in Scottish trews, and carrying the giant white umbrella, joined Mr B with his arm about Pavlova's neck and Mrs B and Olga in long white dresses and eighteenth-century hats, most other visitors mistook them for players in Shakespeare's *A Midsummer Night's Dream*, and could not resist taking photographs. Even the dogs were allowed in this most beautiful of gardens on that halcyon day – by special permission and with all the usual understandings about unfortunate happenings – and Pavlova behaved with all the grace of a prima ballerina.

Their longest jaunt was to Scotland to stay with cousins of Hector who shared two of his three surnames. It was in high summer, the nights shortest and the days longest – particularly in Scotland – and Hector and Olga spent the previous night in Wimbledon so that they could all cram into the Rolls-Royce at half past four in the morning, and be speeding north before all the traffic jams accumulated on the fringes of London. They reached their destination late in the afternoon, a great turreted castle of grey stone looking onto a loch, shouldered by lofty fir trees that broke the winds from the north, and were greeted by a kilted family with plaids over their shoulders and – horror of horrors – a bagpiper whose playing so obviously caused Pavlova acute distress that he had at once to be banished from the scene. Pavlova hung her head and, for what seemed minutes, shook it vigorously, as though trying to empty her ears of the sound, exactly as she might empty them of water had she been ducked in the loch.

'We are,' said their host, 'to pretend as long as you are here, that this is Balmoral and Pavlova is the Queen. We have made a coronet for her, and have brought a couch into the dining room so that at every meal she can recline at the head of the table with her retinue of dogs.' And so, for a long week, Pavlova was indeed the

Queen and all entertainment was arranged for her interest. At breakfast the first morning they brought her milky porridge in a gigantic silver porringer—the biggest ever made, a bowl beyond rarity, unique, made by Alexander Reid, a silversmith in Edinburgh in 1689, the year in which the last Stuart king of Scotland and England was usurped. It weighed one hundred and twenty-three ounces (silver is always measured in ounces) and held a tremendous amount of porridge; with this—that is the porridge—Pavlova clearly fell in love, and so did the dogs, for they licked her cheeks where she had splashed them and then set to licking the porringer clean of every trace.

On most days they climbed onto sleepy old horses and wandered off into the hills, through the forest trees and out on to the moors, with Pavlova in her coronet seeming tiny among them, yet they were gentle with her, never buffeting, adapting to her pace. Walking through the heather was tough for Carrington, the whippet, and Mr B fashioned one of the picnic blankets into a nest between his knees in which she nestled and almost went to sleep, lulled by the motion of the horse's shoulders. They rowed a boat across the loch, Pavlova reclining on the wide seat at the stern, with Hector singing *Loch Lomond* and *Over the Sea to Skye*, and Mr B querulously attempting *The Owl and the Pussycat went to Sea* though he had no firm grasp of either the words or the tune – or even if there was a tune. And one day some Scottish dancers came to entertain them, the music provided by droning fiddles rather than a piper; in their leaping and prancing Pavlova seemed at first to show some interest, even to scrambling to her hooves to stand and watch, but after a while she sidled very discreetly to the door and left the room, returning only when the music and occasional whooping stopped and whisky and delicious shortbread might be had.

But at last came the day when they must again

be up early in the morning and on their way home, and there were hugs and tears, for even the hearts of dour Scots can be moved by the charms of a cultivated donkey. Pavlova should have given back her coronet—a pretty thing of twisted silver wire made by a local smith, but Hector's cousins insisted that she should keep it, for it would fit no human head.

The only calamitous failure among such jaunts occurred when, on a whim, Mr B alone took Pavlova to Golders Green. This he did because he wished her to see the house in which for many years her namesake had lived, Anna Pavlova, the great ballet dancer whose name had sprung into Mr B's mind the moment he first saw the little long-legged donkey in Peshawar. This was Ivy House, clad with ivy as its name suggests, in which she had lived with a menagerie of swans, flamingos and other graceful birds that she imagined might teach her something about the movements of the dance. Mr B, born in the year she had died and prompted by an anniversary, went ill-prepared. He had been to the house as a small child and remembered it as it was then, still with its beautiful birds and a number of cuddly animals, but since then it had been a convalescent home for invalids, a department of the Royal College of Music, a polytechnic college and, eventually (and quite unknown to Mr B) it had become a religious and cultural centre. Mr B, with the help of Hector and the Rolls-Royce, might have been politely welcomed at the gate, but he had crammed poor Pavlova into the back of the Honda that had been the dogs' car before she came to London, very scruffy, with lots of dog-snuffle marks on all the windows and clouds of dog hairs woven into the upholstery. Though tall enough for the dogs she could not stand in it, nor even turn round easily, and was desperate to get out by the time Mr B swept the car through the gates with almost as much panache as Hector's characteristic driving. He opened the hatch and had half unloaded her when a forbidding shadow loomed. 'No donkeys here,' said the voice of the shadow, a uniformed man twice the size of Mr B, 'no equines, no horses, no dogs or crocodiles.' 'But,' said Mr B, 'and no buts either,' said the man. 'But this is Pavlova,' said Mr B, persisting, at which the shadow—who had quite clearly never heard of any Pavlova—raised a monstrous eyebrow and, changing his voice to a sinister whisper, bent low to Mr B's left ear, told him to close the hatch on his damned donkey, get back into his seat—'nice and quiet and drive down the hill as fast as you can.' Mr B then did precisely what was required of him and never again set foot in Golders Green.

In the Village, which is that part of the Wimbledon nearest the Common, Pavlova became a common sight. The old ladies who ran the antique shop always welcomed her with sweets and cakes – not quite as exciting as those of Kahraman Maraş, but perfectly acceptable. She was welcomed at one of the riding stables and the visiting farrier trimmed her hooves when necessary. She was listed as a client at the veterinary surgery, but all that the surgeon had to do was check her heart rate and look at her teeth, for a donkey's contentment in old age is wholly dependent on the condition of teeth that keep on growing until her dying day, perhaps out of alignment, perhaps worn sharp enough to cut her tongue. And in spite of growing muscles where it once seemed that she had none, and putting on a little weight so that she was much less of a waif, she remained a tiny donkey, delicate and a perfect example of her breed, a subgroup of the wild Asiatic Ass.

In summer, when all the doors were open, she often came into the house, particularly when Mr B had visitors, and when Hector and Olga came to lunch or dinner (as they frequently did), no matter what the weather or the time of year, Pavlova was invited to wander into the sitting-room and make herself comfortable on, amongst other things, the fine rugs that Mr B had bought when they were together in Isfahan. But one day Hector and Olga came no more, for he had at last, in the very mountains of Carinthia where he had chosen to travel so slowly with Pavlova and Mr B, driven the old Rolls-Royce too far too fast, misjudged a hairpin bend and tumbled higgledy-piggledy into the ravine below. Mr B thought wryly of the advice once given to Hector always to drive his cars into the ground, for that is exactly what he had now done. Both he and Olga must have been killed instantly, the Austrian police reported – and they also said that they were mightily puzzled by the cache of precious books and manuscripts that had survived unscathed in the car's boot.

Mr B thought often of Hector, his resourcefulness and the Rolls-Royce. Without Hector he might well have had to walk twenty miles a day – and slowly, with Pavlova still a baby and easily exhausted. Without Hector the journey would have been much longer and much more complicated. Without Hector there would have been no sleeping pill, no simple means of smuggling her across the Channel.

Without Hector he might never have succeed-
ed in bringing his donkey home – and for many
years Mr B had a recurring nightmare in which
officials from the Ministry of Agriculture
came knocking on the door, demanding that
he hand over a donkey who had no business to
be here. It was for this reason that, when telling the tale of Pavlova's rescue, he discreetly failed to mention the sleeping pill and the
smuggling, and always told it as though he
had had (somehow, and always without expla-
nation) the necessary papers and certificates
of health. And the more he told the tale – and
this is very odd – the more he regretted that he
had not walked all the way from Peshawar, had
not experienced the extremes of heat and cold,
not suffered the cramps that are the curse of
the walker who has a continent to cross, not
felt his boots or shoes fall to pieces under his
feet, not been able to stop and stare and think
of Alexander the Great driving his Greek army in the contrary direction. Had he been on
foot might he have thought more of young Albrecht Dürer and wise Pieter Bruegel on their
travels south and back again? Might he, like
them, have ridden the Rivers Danube and the
Rhine? – and having thought of them he realised that he could have chugged up the Danube

on a barge all the way from the Black Sea to Ulm in the heart of Europe, through the gorge of the Iron Gate where it separates old Yugoslavia from Rumania, past Budapest and Vienna, Linz and Regensburg, to Ulm, where it is linked by canal to the Rhine. And he imagined a barge on that great river travelling north with the swift current, through one of the most romantic landscapes in all Europe, all the way to the Netherlands and the North Sea – the route that Bruegel surely followed. I must follow it myself one day, thought Mr B but, as is the way of things when a man is no longer young and there is never enough time, he never did.

Time passed – a great deal of it. Carrington, Kahlo and Kollwitz died. Other dogs came, always a whippet, an Alsatian and a mongrel of any old sort, and Mr B almost ran out of names for them. Some became Pavlova's close friends and slept with her as much in the stable as on Mr B's bed, where all dogs were always welcome. One day, when Mr B was feeling a little

old and frail (as, indeed, he really was), he set off for the Common with only Pavlova – no dogs, not even his then Alsatian – and half way there she suddenly dug in her heels and would walk no further – so he took her to the vet instead. 'Nothing obviously wrong,' said that wise man, 'but perhaps the Common is now too much for her. How old is she?' 'Somewhere between twenty-five and thirty,' replied Mr B who was not entirely sure of the year and was by then even worse at simple arithmetic. 'Well there you are – she wants a quieter life.' And if truth be told, so too did Mr B, for he was very close to eighty and often would have been content only to wander round the garden. Younger friends began to take on the task of exercising the dogs, of whom there were now five, for the vet had wished on him an extra whippet and a boxer, whose owner, going abroad, had wanted to have put down. While they were off on the Common Mr B, now leaning as much on Pavlova as she ever leaned on him, together with an older dog or two perhaps, set off, meandering to all four corners of the garden and tottering round the pond if anyone had cut back the overhanging bushes on the further side. In this perambulation Mr B might pick a broken flower, poke the heaps of logs in which intriguing insects lurked, discover that squirrels had stripped the vine of every ripening grape, and tell himself again and again that he must call the tree man to lop this branch and that, once mere twigs but now hefty boughs reaching long and low – but once inside the house again, it always slipped his memory.

It was on the morning of the fourth day of October, the day devoted to St Francis, the saint whom many regard as the patron saint of animals, that Mr B felt unable to leave his bed. Just as the vet, a year or two before, had found nothing wrong with Pavlova, so the doctor could find nothing wrong with Mr B. 'He is tired,' he said to anxious friends and Mrs B, 'let him sleep. Feed him with delicious things. Make sure he drinks a lot.' And so they did, for as the fourth day of October is also, by ancient tradition, the best day to begin making the year's cider from apples and perry from pears, they brought him the finest of both – though it had not been his doctor's intention to make him tipsy.

They also brought Pavlova to his bedside. They dressed her in the saddlebags and sheepskin that he had found for her so long ago in Pakistan, they even discovered her old straw hat, and in the saddlebags they put peaches and pears, ripe bursting figs and pomegranates, and cascades of golden grapes, the sweetest they could find; and she stood stock still by his bed as he reached from his pillows to see what she had brought him. He plucked a grape or two; then, from his open palm, she ate the rest. He ate perhaps a quarter of a fig before surrendering it and another to his Pavlova; three

seeds from the ripest pomegranate followed (and pomegranates, to be sweet, should always ripen on the tree until they split open and are about to fall), and his donkey finished it. It was a pretty pantomime.

That night, at its darkest hour, Pavlova woke, disturbing the two whippets curled against her tummy. For a long moment she stood still, ears pricked and nostrils flared, her nose lifted high, questing the cold air. And then she brayed; it was not the soft bray of welcome uttered when she heard Mr B's car return or when a dog unexpectedly came to see her in her stable, but the repeated bray of anguish and distress, loud enough to wake the household. Everyone came running, except, of course Mr B–and no one wondered at his absence until Pavlova stopped braying and was back on her couch and settled with the whippets. It was then that the last friend to return to his bed thought to see if the hullaballoo had disturbed old Mr B. There was no response to the whispered question, 'Are you awake?' The answer lay in the coolness of the outstretched hand. Very quietly this friend left the room, thinking it best that, after the disturbance with Pavlova, Mrs B should not be roused again, but left in peace to find her husband dead and hold that hand in solitude. And that is exactly what she did; and then she called Mr B's doctor, who was not at all surprised. He, knowing nothing of Pavlova's outburst in the night, entered on the death certificate precisely the moment of her first forlorn bray as the time of her master's death.

The dogs grieved, as dogs do when those who love them die, and so did Pavlova – but she went further, refused to eat and could hardly be persuaded to leave her stable. 'She's very old,' said the vet, who was a new boy at the surgery and had never before had to be doctor to a

donkey – and, indeed, everyone had forgotten just how old she really was; moreover, no one had yet thought of reading Mr B's diary of the year of the great adventure from Pakistan to Wimbledon so many years before. Some three weeks on, in the early hours of the day devoted to St Jude, the patron of lost causes, the household was roused again, this time by the wailing of whippets. Now whippets do not have strong voices and do not use them much, but two are twice as loud as one and their cries from the stable were eventually heard. First one, then the other, feeling cold, had wakened from her tightly curled position against Pavlova's soft and comfortable belly, and each had recognised immediately the reason for the chill. The young vet opined that she had died of old age and that thirty was a good age for a donkey. The whippets, her closest friends among the dogs, knew better. They knew that Pavlova had died of grief.

The obsequies done – Mr B dispatched in a puff of smoke at the local crematorium, Pavlova buried in the garden with his ashes, a young yew tree their shared memorial – Mrs B picked

up her pen, opened Mr B's old diary of thirty years before, and wrote the line:

'Mr B, a wiry little man of fifty with white hair...'

A NOTE ON THE TYPE

The White Umbrella has been set in Monotype Joanna Nova &
Joanna Sans Nova, two digital typefaces derived from the original work of the British artist Eric Gill (1882–1940), acclaimed
in his lifetime as a sculptor, letter-cutter and type designer.

DESIGN & COMPOSITION BY TERRENCE CHOUINARD